To Allie

from

Mrs. W. A. Little

[See page 62

A DUEL WITH AUTOMOBILES

KEEPING UP
WITH
LIZZIE

BY
IRVING BACHELLER

ILLUSTRATED BY
W. H. D. KOERNER

HARPER & BROTHERS PUBLISHERS
NEW YORK AND LONDON
MCMXI

CONTENTS

CHAP.   PAGE

I.   IN WHICH THE LEADING TRADESMEN
      OF POINTVIEW BECOME A BOARD
      OF ASSESSORS   I

II.   IN WHICH LIZZIE RETURNS TO HER
      HOME, HAVING MET A QUEEN AND
      ACQUIRED AN ACCENT AND A
      FIANCÉ   30

III. IN WHICH LIZZIE DESCENDS FROM A
      GREAT HEIGHT   49

IV.   IN WHICH THE HAM WAR HAS ITS
      BEGINNING   74

V.   IN WHICH LIZZIE EXERTS AN INFLU-
      ENCE ON THE AFFAIRS OF THE
      RICH AND GREAT   82

VI.   IN WHICH THE PURSUIT OF LIZZIE
      BECOMES HIGHLY SERIOUS . .   130

VII. IN WHICH THE HONORABLE SOCRATES
      POTTER CATCHES UP WITH LIZZIE   149

ILLUSTRATIONS

A DUEL WITH AUTOMOBILES	*Frontispiece*	
WITH HIS MIND ON THE SUBJECT OF EXTRAVAGANCE	*Facing p.*	4
"SEVEN DOLLARS A BARREL" . . .	"	6
"I WANTED YE TO TELL MR. POTTER ABOUT YER TRAVELS," SAYS SAM .	"	32
LIZZIE DROPPED INTO A CHAIR AN' BEGAN TO CRY	"	52
BILL AN' I GOT TOGETHER OFTEN AN' TALKED OF THE OLD HAPPY DAYS .	"	92
WE SET OUT FOR A TRAMP OVER THE BIG FARM	"	100
"I'M A CANDIDATE FOR NEW HONORS"	"	106
THREE DAYS LATER I DROVE TO THE VILLA	"	112
THE BOY EXERTED HIS CHARMS UPON MY LADY WARBURTON. . . .	"	114
SHE LED US INTO THE BEDROOM . . .	"	124
THEIR EYES WERE WIDE WITH WONDER	"	142

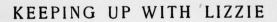

KEEPING UP WITH LIZZIE

KEEPING UP WITH LIZZIE

I

THE Honorable Socrates Potter
was the only "scientific man"
in the village of Pointview, Connecticut. In every point of manhood he
was far ahead of his neighbors. In
a way he had outstripped himself,
for, while his ideas were highly modern, he clung to the dress and man-
ners that prevailed in his youth. He
wore broadcloth every day, and a

choker, and chewed tobacco, and never permitted his work to interfere with the even tenor of his conversation. He loved the old times and fashions, and had a drawling tongue and often spoke in the dialect of his fathers, loving the sound of it. His satirical mood was sure to be flavored with clipped words and changed tenses. The stranger often took him for a "hayseed," but on further acquaintance opened his mouth in astonishment, for Soc. Potter, as many called him, was a man of insight and learning and of a quality of wit herein revealed. He used to call himself "an attorney and peacemaker," but he was more than that. He was the attorney and friend of all his clients, and the philosopher of his community. If one man threatened another with the law in

2

that neighborhood, he was apt to do it in these terms, "We'll see what Soc. Potter has to say about that."

"All right! We'll see," the other would answer, and both parties would be sure to show up at the lawyer's office. Then, probably, Socrates would try his famous lock-and-key expedient. He would sit them down together, lock the door, and say, "Now, boys, I don't believe in getting twelve men for a job that two can do better," and generally he would make them agree.

He had an office over the store of Samuel Henshaw, and made a specialty of deeds, titles, epigrams, and witticisms.

He was a bachelor who called now and then at the home of Miss Betsey Smead, a wealthy spinster of Pointview, but nothing had ever come of it.

He sat with his feet on his desk

and his mind on the subject of extravagance. When he was doing business he sat like other men, but when
his thought assumed a degree of el-
evation his feet rose with it. He
began his story by explaining that it
was all true but the names.

"This is the balloon age," said he,
with a merry twinkle in his gray eyes.
"The inventor has led us into the
skies. The odor of gasoline is in the
path of the eagle. Our thoughts are
between earth and heaven; our prices
have followed our aspirations in the
upward flight. Now here is Sam
Henshaw. Sam? Why, he's a merchant prince o' Pointview — grocery
business—had a girl—name o' Lizzie
—smart and as purty as a wax doll.
Dan Pettigrew, the noblest flower o'
the young manhood o' Pointview, fell
in love with her. No wonder. We

4

WITH HIS MIND ON THE SUBJECT OF EXTRAVAGANCE

were all fond o' Lizzie. They were a han'some couple, an' together about half the time.

"Well, Sam began to aspire, an' nothing would do for Lizzie but the Smythe school at Hardcastle at seven hundred dollars a year. So they rigged her up splendid, an' away she went. From that day she set the pace for this community. Dan had to keep up with Lizzie, and so his father, Bill Pettigrew, sent him to Harvard. Other girls started in the race, an' the first we knew there was a big field in this maiden handicap.

"Well, Sam had been aspirin' for about three months, when he began to perspire. The extras up at Hardcastle had exceeded his expectations. He was goin' a hot pace to keep up with Lizzie, an' it looked as if his morals was meltin' away.

5

"I was in the northern part o' the county one day, an' saw some wonderful, big, red, tasty apples.

"'What ye doin' with yer apples?' says I to the grower.

"'I've sent the most of 'em to Samuel Henshaw, o' Pointview, an' he's sold 'em on commission,' says he.

"'What do ye get for 'em?' I asked.

"'Two dollars an' ten cents a barrel,' says he.

"The next time I went into Sam's store there were the same red apples that came out o' that orchard in the northern part o' the county.

"'How much are these apples?' I says.

"'Seven dollars a barrel,' says Sam.

"'How is it that you get seven dollars a barrel an' only return two dollars an' ten cents to the grower?' I says.

"SEVEN DOLLARS A BARREL"

"Sam stuttered an' changed color. I'd been his lawyer for years, an' I always talked plain to Sam.

"'Wal, the fact is,' says he, with a laugh an' a wink, 'I sold these apples to my clerk.'

"'Sam, ye're wastin' yer talents,' I says. 'Go into the railroad business.'

"Sam was kind o' shamefaced.

"'It costs so much to live I have to make a decent profit somewhere,' says he. 'If you had a daughter to educate, you'd know the reason.'

"I bought a bill o' goods, an' noticed that ham an' butter were up two cents a pound, an' flour four cents a sack, an' other things in proportion. I didn't say a word, but I see that Sam proposed to tax the community for the education o' that Lizzie girl. Folks began to complain, but the tax on each wasn't heavy, an' a good

7

many people owed Sam an' wasn't in shape to quit him. Then Sam had the best store in the village, an' everybody was kind o' proud of it. So we stood this assessment o' Sam's, an' by a general tax paid for the education o' Lizzie. She made friends, an' sailed around in automobiles, an' spent a part o' the Christmas holidays with the daughter o' Mr. Beverly Gottrich on Fifth Avenue, an' young Beverly Gottrich brought her home in his big red runabout. Oh, that was a great day in Pointview!—that red-runabout day of our history when the pitcher was broken at the fountain and they that looked out of the windows trembled.

"Dan Pettigrew was home from Harvard for the holidays, an' he an' Lizzie met at a church party. They held their heads very high, an' seemed

8

to despise each other an' everybody else. Word went around that it was all off between 'em. It seems that they had riz—not risen, but riz—far above each other.

"Now it often happens that when the young ascend the tower o' their aspirations an' look down upon the earth its average inhabitant seems no larger to them than a red ant. Sometimes there's nobody in sight—that is, no real body—nothin' but clouds an' rainbows an' kings an' queens an' their families. Now Lizzie an' Dan were both up in their towers an' lookin' down, an' that was probably the reason they didn't see each other.

"Right away a war began between the rival houses o' Henshaw an' Pettigrew. The first we knew Sam was buildin' a new house with a tower on it — by jingo! — an' hardwood finish inside an' half an acre in the door-yard. The tower was for Lizzie. It signalized her rise in the community. It put her one flight above anybody in Pointview.

"As the house rose, up went Sam's prices again. I went over to the store an' bought a week's provisions, an' when I got the bill I see that he'd taxed me twenty-nine cents for his improvements.

"I met one o' my friends, an' I says to him, 'Wal,' I says, 'Sam is goin' to make us pay for his new house an' lot. Sam's ham an' flour have jumped again. As an assessor Sam is likely to make his mark.'

"'Wal, what do ye expect?' says he. 'Lizzie is in high society, an' he's got to keep up with her. Lizzie must have a home proper to one o' her station. Don't be hard on Sam.'

"'I ain't,' I says. 'But Sam's house ought to be proper to his station instead o' hers.'

"I had just sat down in my office when Bill Pettigrew came in—Sam's great rival in the grocery an' aspiration business. He'd bought a new automobile, an' wanted me to draw a mortgage on his house an' lot for two thousand dollars.

"'You'd better go slow,' I says. 'It looks like bad business to mortgage your home for an automobile.'

"'It's for the benefit o' my customers,' says he.

"'Something purty for 'em to look at?' I asked.

"'It will quicken deliveries,' says he.

"'You can't afford it,' I says.

"'Yes, I can,' says he. 'I've put up prices twenty per cent., an' it

11

ain't agoin' to bother me to pay for it.'

"'Oh, then your customers are goin' to pay for it!' I says, 'an' you're only a guarantor.'

"'I wouldn't put it that way,' says he. 'It costs more to live these days. Everything is goin' up.'

"'Includin' taxes,' I says to Bill, an' went to work an' drew his mortgage for him, an' he got his automobile.

"I'd intended to take my trade to his store, but when I saw that he planned to tax the community for his luxuries I changed my mind and went over to Eph Hill's. He kept the only other decent grocery store in the village. His prices were just about on a level with the others.

"'How do you explain it that prices have gone up so?' I asked.

"'Why, they say it's due to an overproduction o' gold,' says he.

"'Looks to me like an overproduction of argument,' I says. 'The old Earth keeps shellin' out more gold ev'ry year, an' the more she takes out o' her pockets the more I have to take out o' mine.'

"Wal, o' course I had to keep in line, so I put up the prices o' my work a little to be in fashion. Everybody kicked good an' plenty, an' nobody worse'n Sam an' Bill an' Ephraim, but I told 'em how I'd read that there was so much gold in the world it kind o' set me hankerin'.

"Ye know I had ten acres o' worn-out land in the edge o' the village, an' while others bought automobiles an' such luxuries I invested in fertilizers an' hired a young man out of an agricultural school an' went to farm-

13

in'. Within a year I was raisin' all the meat an' milk an' vegetables that I needed, an' sellin' as much ag'in to my neighbors.

"Well, Pointview under Lizzie was like Rome under Theodora. The immorals o' the people throve an' grew. As prices went up decency went down, an' wisdom rose in value like meat an' flour. Seemed so everybody that had a dollar in the bank an' some that didn't bought automobiles. They kept me busy drawin' contracts an' deeds an' mortgages an' searchin' titles, an' o' course I prospered. More than half the population converted property into cash an' cash into folly —automobiles, piano-players, foreign tours, vocal music, modern languages, an' the aspirations of other people. They were puttin' it on each other. Every man had a deep scheme for

14

makin' the other fellow pay for his fun. Reminds me o' that verse from Zechariah, 'I will show them no mercy, saith the Lord, but I will deliver every man into the hand of his neighbor.' Now the baron business has generally been lucrative, but here in Pointview there was too much competition. We were all barons. Everybody was taxin' everybody else for his luxuries, an' nobody could save a cent—nobody but me an' Eph Hill. He didn't buy any automobiles or build a new house or send his girl to the seminary. He kept both feet on the ground, but he put up his prices along with the rest. By-an'-by Eph had a mortgage on about half the houses in the village. That showed what was the matter with the other men.

"The merchants all got liver-complaint. There were twenty men that I used to see walkin' home to their dinner every day or down to the post-office every evenin'. But they didn't walk any more. They scud along in their automobiles at twenty miles an hour, with the whole family around 'em. They looked as if they thought that now at last they were keepin' up with Lizzie. Their homes were empty most o' the time. The reading-lamp was never lighted. There was no season o' social converse. Every merchant but Eph Hill grew fat an' round, an' complained of indigestion an' sick-headache. Sam looked like a moored balloon. Seemed so their morals grew fat an' flabby an' shif'-less an' in need of exercise. Their morals travelled too, but they travelled from mouth to mouth, as ye might say, an' very fast. More'n half

16

of 'em give up church an' went off on the country roads every Sunday. All along the pike from Pointview to Jerusalem Corners ye could see where they'd laid humbly on their backs in the dust, prayin' to a new god an' tryin' to soften his heart with oil or open the gates o' mercy with a monkey-wrench.

"Bill came into my shop one day an' looked as if he hadn't a friend in the world. He wanted to borrow some money.

"'Money!' I says. 'What makes ye think I've got money?'

"'Because ye ain't got any automobile,' he says, laughin'.

"'No,' I says. 'You bought one, an' that was all I could afford.'

"It never touched him. He went on as dry as a duck in a shower. 'You're one o' the few sensible men

17

in this village. You live within yer means, an' you ought to have money if ye ain't.'

"'I've got a little, but I don't see why you should have it,' I says. 'You want me to do all the savin' for both of us.'

"'It costs so much to live I can't save a cent,' he says. 'You know I've got a boy in college, an' it costs fearful. I told my boy the other day how I worked my way through school an' lived on a dollar a week in a little room an' did my own washin'. He says to me, " Well, Governor, you forget that I have a social position to maintain."'

"'He's right,' I says. 'You can't expect him to belong to the varsity crew an' the Dickey an' the Hasty-Puddin' Club an' dress an' behave like the son of an ordinary grocer in

Pointview, Connecticut. Ye can't live on nuts an' raisins an' be decent in such a position. Looks to me as if it would require the combined incomes o' the grocer an' his lawyer to maintain it. His position is likely to be hard on your disposition. He's tryin' to keep up with Lizzie—that's what's the matter.'

"For a moment Bill looked like a lost dog. I told him how Grant an' Thomas stood on a hilltop one day an' saw their men bein' mowed down like grass, an' by-an'-by Thomas says to Grant, 'Wal, General, we'll have to move back a little; it's too hot for the boys here.'

"'I'm afraid your boy's position is kind of uncomf'table,' I says.

"'I'll win out,' he says. 'My boy will marry an' settle down in a year or so, then he'll begin to help me.'

19

"'But you may be killed off before then,' I says.

"'If my friends 'll stand by me I'll pull through,' says he.

"'But your friends have their own families to stand by,' I says.

"'Look here, Mr. Potter,' says he. 'You've no such expense as I have. You're able to help me, an' you ought to. I've got a note comin' due to-morrow an' no money to pay it with.'

"'Renew it an' then retrench,' I says. 'Cut down your expenses an' your prices.'

"'Can't,' says he. 'It costs too much to live. What 'll I do?'

"'You ought to die,' I says, very mad.

"'I can't,' says he.

"'Why not?'

"'It costs so much to die,' he says.

20

'Why, it takes a thousan' dollars to give a man a decent funeral these days.'

"'Wal,' I says, 'a man that can't afford either to live or die excites my sympathy an' my caution. You've taxed the community for yer luxuries, an' now ye want to tax me for yer notes. It's unjust discrimination. It gives me a kind of a lonesome feelin'. You tell your boy Dan to come an' see me. He needs advice more than you need money, an' I've got a full line of it.'

"Bill went away richer by a check for a few hundred dollars. Oh, I always know when I'm losin' money! I'm not like other citizens o' Pointview.

"Dan came to see me the next Saturday night. He was a big, blue-eyed, handsome, good-natured boy, an' dressed like the son of a million-

21

aire. I brought him here to the office, an' he sat down beside me.

"'Dan,' I says, 'what are your plans for the future?'

"'I mean to be a lawyer,' says he.

"'Quit it,' I says.

"'Why?' says he.

"'There are too many lawyers. We don't need any more. They're devourin' our substance.'

"'What do you suggest?'

"'Be a real man. We're on the verge of a social revolution. Boys have been leaving the farms an' going into the cities to be grand folks. The result is we have too many grand folks an' too few real folks. The tide has turned. Get aboard.'

"'I don't understand you.'

"'America needs wheat an' corn an' potatoes more than it needs arguments an' theories.'

"'Would you have me be a farmer?' he asked, in surprise.

"'A farmer!' I says. 'It's a new business—an exact science these days. Think o' the high prices an' the cheap land with its productiveness more than doubled by modern methods. The country is longing for big, brainy men to work its idle land. Soon we shall not produce enough for our own needs.'

"'But I'm too well educated to be a farmer,' says he.

"'Pardon me,' I says. 'The land 'll soak up all the education you've got an' yell for more. Its great need is education. We've been sending the smart boys to the city an' keeping the fools on the farm. We've put everything on the farm but brains. That's what's the matter with the farm.'

23

"'But farming isn't dignified,' says Dan.

"'Pardon me ag'in,' says I. 'It's more dignified to search for the secrets o' God in the soil than to grope for the secrets o' Satan in a lawsuit. Any fool can learn Blackstone an' Kent an' Greenleaf, but the book o' law that's writ in the soil is only for keen eyes.'

"'I want a business that fits a gentleman,' says Dan.

"'An' the future farmer can be as much of a gentleman as God 'll let him,' says I. 'He'll have as many servants as his talents can employ. His income will exceed the earnings o' forty lawyers taken as they average. His position will be like that o' the rich planter before the war.'

"'Well, how shall I go about it?' he says, half convinced.

"'First stop tryin' to keep up with

24

Lizzie,' says I. 'The way to beat Lizzie is to go toward the other end o' the road. Ye see, you've dragged yer father into the race, an' he's about winded. Turn around an' let Lizzie try to keep up with you. Second, change yer base. Go to a school of agriculture an' learn the business just as you'd go to a school o' law or medicine. Begin modest. Live within yer means. If you do right I'll buy you all the land ye want an' start ye goin'.'

"When he left I knew that I'd won my case. In a week or so he sent me a letter saying that he'd decided to take my advice.

"He came to see me often after that. The first we knew he was goin' with Marie Benson. Marie had a reputation for good sense, but right away she began to take after Lizzie, an' struck a tolerably good pace.

Went to New York to study music an' perfect herself in French.

"I declare it seemed as if about every girl in the village was tryin' to be a kind of a princess with a full-jewelled brain. Girls who didn't know an adjective from an adverb an' would have been stuck by a simple sum in algebra could converse in French an' sing in Italian. Not one in ten was willin', if she knew how, to sweep a floor or cook a square meal. Their souls were above it. Their feet were in Pointview an' their heads in Dreamland. They talked o' the doin's o' the Four Hundred an' the successes o' Lizzie. They trilled an' warbled; they pounded the family piano; they golfed an' motored an' whisted; they engaged in the titivation of toy dogs an' the cultivation o' general debility; they ate caramels an' chocolates

26

enough to fill up a well; they complained; they dreamed o' sunbursts an' tiaras while their papas worried about notes an' bills; they lay on downy beds of ease with the last best seller, an' followed the fortunes of the bold youth until he found his treasure at last in the unhidden chest of the heroine; they created what we are pleased to call the servant problem, which is really the drone problem, caused by the added number who toil not, but have to be toiled for; they grew in fat an' folly. Some were both ox-eyed an' peroxide. Homeliness was to them the only misfortune, fat the only burden, and pimples the great enemy of woman.

"Now the organs of the human body are just as shiftless as the one that owns 'em. The systems o' these fair ladies couldn't do their own work. The physician an' the surgeon were added to the list o' their servants, an' became as necessary as the cook an' the chambermaid. But they were keeping up with Lizzie. Poor things! They weren't so much to blame. They thought their fathers were rich, an' their fathers enjoyed an' clung to that reputation. They hid their poverty an' flaunted the flag of opulence.

"It costs money, big money an' more, to produce a generation of invalids. The fathers o' Pointview had paid for it with sweat an' toil an' broken health an' borrowed money an' the usual tax added to the price o' their goods or their labor. Then one night the cashier o' the First National Bank blew out his brains. We found that he had stolen eighteen thousand dollars in the effort to keep up. That was a lesson to the Lizzie-chasers! Why, sir, we found that each of his older girls had diamond rings an' could sing in three languages, an' a boy was in college. Poor man! he didn't steal for his own pleasure. Everything went at auction—house, grounds, rings, automobile. Another man was caught sellin' under weight with fixed scales, an' went to prison. Henry Brown failed, an' we found that he had borrowed five hundred dollars from John Bass, an' at the same time John Bass had borrowed six hundred from Tom Rogers, an' Rogers had borrowed seven hundred an' fifty from Sam Henshaw, an' Henshaw had borrowed the same amount from Percival Smith, an' Smith had got it from me. The chain broke, the note structure fell like a house o' cards, an' I was the only loser—think o' that. There were five capitalists an' only one man with real money.

II

IN WHICH LIZZIE RETURNS TO HER
HOME, HAVING MET A QUEEN AND
ACQUIRED AN ACCENT AND
A FIANCÉ

"SAM HENSHAW'S girl had grad-
uated an' gone abroad with her
mother. One Sunday 'bout a year
later, Sam flew up to the door o' my
house in his automobile. He lit on
the sidewalk an' struggled up the steps
with two hundred an' forty-seven
pounds o' meat on him. He walked
like a man carryin' a barrel o' pork.
He acted as if he was glad to see me
an' the big arm-chair on the piaz'.

"'What's the news?' I asked.

"'Lizzie an' her mother got back this mornin',' he gasped. 'They've been six months in Europe. Lizzie is in love with it. She's hobnobbed with kings an' queens. She talks art beautiful. I wish you'd come over an' hear her hold a conversation. It's wonderful. She's goin' to be a great addition to this community. She's got me faded an' on the run. I ran down to the store for a few minutes this mornin', an' when I got back she says to me:

"'"Father, you always smell o' ham an' mustard. Have you been in that disgusting store? Go an' take a bahth at once." That's what she called it—a "bahth." Talks just like the English people—she's been among 'em so long. Get into my car an' I'll take ye over an' fetch ye back.'

"Sam regarded his humiliation with

3   31

pride an' joy. At last Lizzie had convinced him that her education had paid. My curiosity was excited. I got in an' we flew over to his house. Sam yelled up the stairway kind o' joyful as we come in, an' his wife answered at the top o' the stairs an' says:

"'Mr. Henshaw, I wish you wouldn't shout in this house like a boy calling the cows.'

"I guess she didn't know I was there. Sam ran up-stairs an' back, an' then we turned into that splendid parlor o' his an' set down. Purty soon Liz an' her mother swung in an' smiled very pleasant an' shook hands an' asked how was my family, etc., an' went right on talkin'. I saw they didn't ask for the purpose of gettin' information. Liz was dressed to kill an' purty as a picture—cheeks red as a rooster's comb an' waist like a

32

"I WANTED YE TO TELL MR. POTTER ABOUT YER TRAVELS," SAYS SAM

hornet's. The cover was off her show-case, an' there was a diamond sun-burst in the middle of it, an' the jewels were surrounded by charms to which I am not wholly insensible even now.

"'I wanted ye to tell Mr. Potter about yer travels,' says Sam.

"Lizzie smiled an' looked out o' the window a minute an' fetched a sigh an' struck out, lookin' like Deacon Bristow the day he give ten dollars to the church. She told about the cities an' the folks an' the weather in that queer, English way she had o' talkin'.

"'Tell how ye hobnobbed with the Queen o' Italy,' Sam says.

"'Oh, father! Hobnobbed!' says she. 'Anybody would think that she and I had manicured each other's hands. She only spoke a few words of Italian and looked very gracious an' beautiful an' complimented my color.'

33

"Then she lay back in her chair, kind o' weary, an' Sam asked me how was business—just to fill in the gap, I guess. Liz woke up an' showed how far she'd got ahead in the race.

"'Business!' says she, with animation. 'That's why I haven't any patience with American men. They never sit down for ten minutes without talking business. Their souls are steeped in commercialism. Don't you see how absurd it is, father? There are plenty of lovely things to talk about.'

"Sam looked guilty, an' I felt sorry for him. It had cost heavy to educate his girl up to a p'int where she could give him so much advice an' information. The result was natural. She was irritated by the large cubic capacity — the length, breadth, and thickness of his ignorance and unrefinement; he was dazed by the length, breadth, an' thickness of her learning an' her charm. He didn't say a word. He bowed his head before this pretty, perfumed casket of erudition.

"'You like Europe,' I says.

"'I love it,' says she. 'It's the only place to live. There one finds so much of the beautiful in art and music and so many cultivated people.'

"Lizzie was a handsome girl, an' had more sense than any o' the others that tried to keep up with her. After all, she was Sam's fault, an' Sam was a sin conceived an' committed by his wife, as ye might say. She had made him what he was.

"'Have you seen Dan Pettigrew lately?' Lizzie asked.

"'Yes,' I says. 'Dan is goin' to be a farmer.'

"'A farmer!' says she, an' covered

35

her face with her handkerchief an'
shook with merriment.

"'Yes,' I says. 'Dan has come
down out o' the air. He's abandoned
folly. He wants to do something to
help along.'

"'Yes, of course,' says Lizzie, in a
lofty manner. 'Dan is really an excellent boy—isn't he?'

"'Yes, an' he's livin' within his
means—that's the first mile-stone in
the road to success,' I says. 'I'm
goin' to buy him a thousand acres o'
land, an' one o' these days he'll own
it an' as much more. You wait.
He'll have a hundred men in his employ, an' flocks an' herds an' a market
of his own in New York. He'll con-
trol prices in this county, an' they're
goin' down. He'll be a force in the
State.'

"They were all sitting up. The

36

faces o' the Lady Henshaw an' her daughter turned red.

"'I'm very glad to hear it, I'm sure,' said her Ladyship.

"I wasn't so sure o' that as she was, an' there, for me, was the milk in the cocoanut. I was joyful.

"'Why, it's perfectly lovely!' says Lizzie, as she fetched her pretty hands together in her lap.

"'Yes, you want to cultivate Dan,' I says. 'He's a man to be reckoned with.'

"'Oh, indeed!' says her Ladyship.

"'Yes, indeed!' I says, 'an' the girls are all after him.'

"I just guessed that. I knew it was unscrupulous, but livin' here in this atmosphere does affect the morals even of a lawyer. Lizzie grew red in the face.

"'He could marry one o' the Four Hundred if he wanted to,' I says.

37

'The other evening he was seen in the big red tourin'-car o' the Van Alstynes. What do you think o' that?'

"Now that was true, but the chauffeur had been a college friend o' Dan's, an' I didn't mention that.

"Lizzie had a dreamy smile in her face.

"'Why, it's wonderful!' says she. 'I didn't know he'd improved so.'

"'I hear that his mother is doing her own work,' says the Lady Henshaw, with a forced smile.

"'Yes, think of it,' I says. 'The woman is earning her daily bread—actually helpin' her husband. Did you ever hear o' such a thing! I'll have to scratch 'em off my list. It's too uncommon. It ain't respectable.'

"Her Ladyship began to suspect me an' retreated with her chin in the air. She'd had enough.

" I thought that would do an' drew out o' the game. Lizzie looked confident. She seemed to have something up her sleeve besides that lovely arm o' hers.

"I went home, an' two days later Sam looked me up again. Then the secret came out o' the bag. He'd heard that I had some money in the savings - banks over at Bridgeport payin' me only three and a half per cent., an' he wanted to borrow it an' pay me six per cent. His generosity surprised me. It was not like Sam.

"'What's the matter with you?' I asked. 'Is it possible that your profits have all gone into gasoline an' rubber an' silk an' education an' hardwood finish an' human fat?'

"'Well, it costs so much to live,' he says, 'an' the wholesalers have kept

39

liftin' the prices on me. Now there's the meat trust—their prices are up thirty-five per cent.'

"'Of course,' I says, 'the directors have to have their luxuries. You taxed us for yer new house an' yer automobile an' yer daughter's education, an' they're taxin' you for their steam-yachts an' private cars an' racin' stables. You can't expect to do all the taxin'. The wholesalers learnt about the profits that you an' others like ye was makin', an' they concluded that they needed a part of 'em. Of course they had to have their luxuries, an' they're taxin' you —they couldn't afford to have 'em if they didn't. Don't complain.'

"'I'll come out all right,' he says. 'I'm goin' to raise my whole schedule fifteen per cent.'

"'The people won't stand it—they

can't,' says I. 'You'll be drownin'
the miller. They'll leave you.'

"'It won't do 'em any good,' says
he. 'Bill an' Eph will make their
prices agree with mine.'

"'Folks will go back to the land,
as I have,' says I.

"'They don't know enough,' says
Sam. 'Farmin' is a lost art here in
the East. You take my word for it
—they'll pay our prices—they'll have
to—an' the rich folks, they don't
worry about prices. I pay a commission to every steward an' butler
in this neighborhood.'

"'I won't help you,' says I. 'It's
wicked. You ought to have saved
your money.'

"'In a year from now I'll have
money to burn,' he says. 'For one
thing, my daughter's education is
finished, an' that has cost heavy.'

"'How much would it cost to unlearn it?' I asked. 'That's goin' to cost more than it did to get it, I'm 'fraid. In my opinion the first thing to do with her is to uneducate her.'

"That was like a red-hot iron to Sam. It kind o' het him up.

"'Why, sir, you don't appreciate her,' says he. 'That girl is far above us all here in Pointview. She's a queen.'

"'Well, Sam,' I says, 'if there's anything you don't need just now it's a queen. If I were you I wouldn't graft that kind o' fruit on the grocery-tree. Hams an' coronets don't flourish on the same bush. They have a different kind of a bouquet. They don't harmonize. Then, Sam, what do you want of a girl that's far above ye? Is it any comfort to you to be despised in your own home?'

42

"'Mr. Potter, I haven't educated her for my own home or for this community, but for higher things,' says Sam.

"'You hairy old ass! The first you know,' I says, 'they'll have your skin off an' layin' on the front piaz' for a door-mat.'

"Sam started for the open air. I hated to be ha'sh with him, but he needed some education himself, an' it took a beetle an' wedge to open his mind for it. He lifted his chin so high that the fat swelled out on the back of his neck an' unbuttoned his collar. Then he turned an' said: 'My daughter is too good for this town, an' I don't intend that she shall stay here. She has been asked to marry a man o' fortune in the old country.'

"'So I surmised, an' I suppose you find that the price o' husbands has gone up,' I says.

43

"Sam didn't answer me.

"'They want you to settle some money on the girl—don't they?' I asked.

"'My wife says it's the custom in the old country,' says Sam.

"'Suppose he ain't worth the price?'

"'They say he's a splendid fellow,' says Sam.

"'You let me investigate him,' I says, 'an' if he's really worth the price I'll help ye to pay it.'

"Sam said that was fair, an' thanked me for the offer, an' gave me the young man's address. He was a Russian by the name of Alexander Rolanoff, an' Sam insisted that he belonged to a very old family of large means an' noble blood, an' said that the young man would be in Pointview that summer. I wrote to

44

the mayor of the city in which he was said to live, but got no answer.

"Alexander came. He was a costly an' beautiful young man, about thirty years old, with red cheeks an' curly hair an' polished finger - nails, an' wrote poetry. Sometimes ye meet a man that excites yer worst suspicions. Your right hand no sooner lets go o' his than it slides down into your pocket to see if anything has happened; or maybe you take the arm o' yer wife or yer daughter an' walk away. Aleck leaned a little in both directions. But, sir, Sam didn't care to know my opinion of him. Never said another word to me on the subject, but came again to ask about the money.

"'Look here, Sam,' I says. 'You tell Lizzie that I want to have a talk with her at four o'clock in this office?

45

If she really wants to buy this man, I'll see what can be done about it.'

"'All right, you talk with her,' says he, an' went out.

"In a few minutes Dan showed up.

"'Have you seen Lizzie?' says I.

"'Not to speak to her,' says Dan. 'Looks fine, doesn't she?'

"'Beautiful!' I says. 'How is Marie Benson?'

"'Oh, the second time I went to see her she was trying to keep up with Lizzie,' says he. 'She's changed her gait. Was going to New York after a lot o' new frills. I suppose she thought that I wanted a grand lady. That's the trouble with all the girls here. A man might as well marry the real thing as an imitation. I wish Lizzie would get down off her high horse.'

"'She's goin' to swap him for one

46

with still longer legs,' I says. 'Lizzie
is engaged to a gentleman o' fortune
in the old country.'

"Dan's face began to stretch out
long as if it was made of injy-rubber.

"'It's too bad,' says he. 'Lizzie is
a good-hearted girl, if she is spoilt.'

"'Fine girl!' I says. 'An', Dan, I
was in hopes that she would discover
her own folly before it was too late.
But she saw that others had begun
to push her in the race an' that she
had to let out another link or fall
behind.'

"'Well, I wish her happiness,' says
Dan, with a sigh.

"'Go an' tell her so,' I says. 'Show
her that you have some care as to
whether she lives or dies.'

"I could see that his feelin's had
been honed 'til they were sharp as a
razor.

"'I've seen that fellow,' he says, 'an' he'll never marry Lizzie if I can prevent it. I hate the looks of him. I shall improve the first opportunity I have to insult him.'

"'That might be impossible,' I suggested.

"'But I'll make the effort,' says Dan.

"As an insulter I wouldn't wonder if Dan had large capacity when properly stirred up.

"'Better let him alone. I have lines out that will bring information. Be patient.'

"Dan rose and said he would see me soon, an' left with a rather stern look in his face.

III

IN WHICH LIZZIE DESCENDS FROM A GREAT HEIGHT

"LIZZIE was on hand at the hour appointed. We sat down here all by ourselves.

"'Lizzie,' I says, 'why in the world did you go to Europe for a husband? It's a slight to Pointview—a discouragement of home industry.'

"'There was nobody here that seemed to want me,' she says, blushin' very sweet.

"She had dropped her princess manner an' seemed to be ready for straight talk.

"'If that's so, Lizzie, it's your fault,' I says.

"'I don't understand you,' says she.

"'Why, my dear child, it's this way,' I says. 'Your mother an' father have meant well, but they've been foolish. They've educated you for a millionairess, an' all that's lackin' is the millions. You overawed the boys here in Pointview. They thought that you felt above 'em, whether you did or not; an' the boys on Fifth Avenue were glad to play with you, but they didn't care to marry you. I say it kindly, Lizzie, an' I'm a friend o' yer father's, an' you can afford to let me say what I mean. Those young fellows wanted the millions as well as the millionairess. One of our boys fell in love with ye an' tried to keep up, but your pace was too hot for him. His father got in trouble, an' the boy had to drop out. Every well-born girl in

50

the village entered the race with ye.
An era of extravagance set in that
threatened the solvency, the honor,
o' this sober old community. Their
fathers had to borrow money to keep
agoin'. They worked overtime, they
importuned their creditors, they wal-
lowed in low finance while their
daughters revelled in the higher walks
o' life an' sang in different languages.
Even your father—I tell you in con-
fidence, for I suppose he wouldn't
have the courage to do it—is in financial difficulties. Now, Lizzie, I want
to be kind to you, for I believe you're
a good girl at heart, but you ought
to know that all this is what your
accomplishments have accomplished.'

"She rose an' walked across the
room, with trembling lips. She had
seized her parachute an' jumped from
her balloon and was slowly approach-

in' the earth. I kept her comin'. 'These clothes an' jewels that you wear, Lizzie—these silks an' laces, these sunbursts an' solitaires—don't seem to harmonize with your father's desire to borrow money. Pardon me, but I can't make 'em look honest. They are not paid for—or if they are they are paid for with other men's money. They seem to accuse you. They'd accuse me if I didn't speak out plain to ye.'

"All of a sudden Lizzie dropped into a chair an' began to cry. She had lit safely on the ground.

"It made me feel like a murderer, but it had to be. Poor girl! I wanted to pick her up like a baby an' kiss her. It wasn't that I loved Lizzie less but Rome more. She wasn't to blame. Every spoilt woman stands for a fool-man. Most o' them need—

LIZZIE DROPPED INTO A CHAIR AN' BEGAN TO CRY

not a master—but a frank counsellor. I locked the door. She grew calm an' leaned on my table, her face covered with her hands. My clock shouted the seconds in the silence. Not a word was said for two or three minutes.

"'I have been brutal,' I says, by-an'-by. 'Forgive me.'

"'Mr. Potter,' she says, 'you've done me a great kindness. I'll never forget it. What shall I do?'

"'Well, for one thing,' says I, 'go back to your old simplicity an' live within your means.'

"'I'll do it,' she says; 'but—I—I supposed my father was rich. Oh, I wish we could have had this talk before!'

"'Did you know that Dan Pettigrew was in love with you?' I put it straight from the shoulder. 'He wouldn't dare tell ye, but you ought to know it. You are regarded as a

53

kind of a queen here, an' it's cus-
tomary for queens to be approached
by ambassadors.'

"Her face lighted up.

"'In love with me?' she whispered.
'Why, Mr. Potter, I never dreamed of
such a thing. Are you sure? How do
you know? I thought he felt above me.'

"'An' he thought you felt above
him,' I says.

"'How absurd! how unfortunate!'
she whispered. 'I couldn't marry
him now if he asked me. This thing
has gone too far. I wouldn't treat
any man that way.'

"'You are engaged to Alexander,
are you?' I says.

"'Well, there is a sort of under-
standing, and I think we are to be
married if—if—'

"She paused, and tears came to
her eyes again.

54

"'You are thinking o' the money,' says I.

"'I am thinking o' the money,' says she. 'It has been promised to him. He will expect it.'

"'Do you think he is an honest man? Will he treat you well?'

"'I suppose so.'

"'Then let me talk with him. Perhaps he would take you without anything to boot.'

"'Please don't propose that,' says she. 'I think he's getting the worst of it now. Mr. Potter, would you lend *me* the money? I ask it because I don't want the family to be disgraced or Mr. Rolanoff to be badly treated. He is to invest the money in my name in a very promising venture. He says he can double it within three months.'

"It would have been easy for me

55

to laugh, but I didn't. Lizzie's attitude in the whole matter pleased me. I saw that her heart was sound. I promised to have a talk with her father and see her again. I looked into his affairs carefully and put him on a new financial basis with a loan of fifteen thousand dollars.

"One day he came around to my office with Alexander an' wanted me to draw up a contract between him an' the young man. It was a rather crude proposition, an' I laughed, an' Aleck sat with a bored smile on his face.

"'Oh, if he's good enough for your daughter,' I said, 'his word ought to be good enough for you.'

"'That's all right,' says Sam, 'but business is business. I want it down in black an' white that the income from this money is to be paid to my daughter, and that neither o' them shall make any further demand on me.'

"Well, I drew that fool contract, an', after it was signed, Sam delivered ten one-thousand-dollar bills to the young man, who was to become his son-in-law the following month with the assistance of a caterer and a florist and a string - band, all from New Haven.

"Within half an hour Dan Pettigrew came roarin' up in front o' my office in the big red automobile of his father's. In a minute he came in to see me. He out with his business soon as he lit in a chair.

"'I've learned that this man Rolanoff is a scoundrel,' says he.

"'A scoundrel!' says I.

"'Of purest ray serene,' says he.

"I put a few questions, but he'd

nothing in the way o' proof to offer
—it was only the statement of a
newspaper.

"'Is that all you know against
him?' I asked.

"'He won't fight,' says Dan. 'I've
tried him—I've begged him to fight.'

"'Well, I've got better evidence
than you have,' I says. 'It came a
few minutes before you did.'

"I showed him a cablegram from a
London barrister that said:

"'Inquiry complete. The man is
a pure adventurer, character *nil.*'

"'We must act immediately,' says
Dan.

"'I have telephoned all over the
village for Sam,' I says. 'They say
he's out in his car with Aleck an'
Lizzie. I asked them to send him
here as soon as he returns.'

"'They're down on the Post Road.

I met 'em on my way here,' says Dan. 'We can overtake that car easy.'

"Well, the wedding - day was approaching an' Aleck had the money, an' the thought occurred to me that he might give 'em the slip somewhere on the road an' get away with it. I left word in the store that if Sam got back before I saw him he was to wait with Aleck in my office until I returned, an' off we started like a baseball on its way from the box to the catcher.

"An officer on his motor-cycle overhauled us on the Post Road. He knew me.

"'It's a case o' sickness,' I says, 'an' we're after Sam Henshaw.'

"'He's gone down the road an' hasn't come back yet,' says the officer.

"I passed him a ten-dollar bill.

"'Keep within sight of us,' I says. 'We may need you any minute.'

"He nodded and smiled, an' away we went.

"'I'm wonderin' how we're agoin' to get the money,' I says, havin' told Dan about it.

"'I'll take it away from him,' says Dan.

"'That wouldn't do,' says I.

"'Why not?'

"'Why not!' says I. 'You wouldn't want to be arrested for highway robbery. Then, too, we must think o' Lizzie. Poor girl! It's agoin' to be hard on her, anyhow. I'll try a bluff. It's probable that he's worked this game before. If so, we can rob him without violence an' let him go.'

"Dan grew joyful as we sped along.

"'Lizzie is mine,' he says. 'She wouldn't marry him now.'

"He told me how fond they had been of each other until they got accomplishments an' began to put up the price o' themselves. He said that in their own estimation they had riz in value like beef an' ham, an' he confessed how foolish he had been. We were excited an' movin' fast.

"'Something 'll happen soon,' he says.

"An' it did, within ten minutes from date. We could see a blue car half a mile ahead.

"'I'll go by that ol' freight-car o' the Henshaws',' says Dan. 'They'll take after me, for Sam is vain of his car. We can halt them in that narrow cut on the hill beyond the Byron River.'

"We had rounded the turn at Chesterville, when we saw the Henshaw car just ahead of us, with Aleck at

the wheel an' Lizzie beside him an'
Sam on the back seat. I saw the
peril in the situation.

"The long rivalry between the
houses of Henshaw an' Pettigrew,
reinforced by that of the young men,
was nearing its climax.

"'See me go by that old soap-box
o' the Henshaws',' says Dan, as he
pulled out to pass 'em.

"Then Dan an' Aleck began a duel
with automobiles. Each had a forty-
horse-power engine in his hands, with
which he was resolved to humble the
other. Dan knew that he was goin'
to bring down the price o' Alecks an'
Henshaws. First we got ahead; then
they scraped by us, crumpling our
fender on the nigh side. Lizzie an'
I lost our hats in the scrimmage.
We gathered speed an' ripped off a
section o' their bulwarks, an' roared

62

along neck an' neck with 'em. The broken fenders rattled like drums in a battle. A hen flew up an' hit me in the face, an' came nigh unhorsin' me. I hung on. It seemed as if Fate was tryin' to halt us, but our horse-power was too high. A dog went under us. It began to rain a little. We were a length ahead at the turn by the Byron River. We swung for the bridge an' skidded an' struck a telephone pole, an' I went right on over the stone fence an' the clay bank an' lit on my head in the water. Dan Pettigrew lit beside me. Then came Lizzie an' Sam—they fairly rained into the river. I looked up to see if Aleck was comin', but he wasn't. Sam, bein' so heavy, had stopped quicker an' hit in shallow water near the shore, but, as luck would have it, the bottom was soft an' he had come down feet foremost, an' a broken leg an' some bad bruises were all he could boast of. Lizzie was in hysterics, but seemed to be unhurt. Dan an' I got 'em out on the shore, an' left 'em cryin' side by side, an' scrambled up the bank to find Aleck. He had aimed too low an' hit the wall, an' was stunned, an' apparently, for the time, dead as a herrin' on the farther side of it. I removed the ten one-thousand-dollar bills from his person to prevent complications an' tenderly laid him down. Then he came to very sudden.

"'Stop!' he murmured. 'You're robbin' me.'

"'Well, you begun it,' I says. 'Don't judge me hastily. I'm a philanthropist. I'm goin' to leave you yer liberty an' a hundred dollars. You take it an' get. If you ever return to Connecticut I'll arrest you at sight.'

"I gave him the money an' called the officer, who had just come up. A traveller in a large tourin'-car had halted near us.

"'Put him into that car an' take him to Chesterville,' I said.

"He limped to the car an' left without a word.

"I returned to my friends an' gently broke the news.

"Sam blubbered. 'Education done it,' says he, as he mournfully shook his head.

"'Yes,' I says. 'Education is responsible for a damned lot of ignorance.'

"'An' some foolishness,' says Sam, as he scraped the mud out of his hair. 'Think of our goin' like that. We ought to have known better.'

"'We knew better,' I says, 'but we had to keep up with Lizzie.'

"Sam turned toward Lizzie an' moaned in a broken voice, 'I wish it had killed me.'

"'Why so?' I asked.

"'It costs so much to live,' Sam sobbed, in a half-hysterical way. 'I've got an expensive family on my hands.'

"'You needn't be afraid o' havin' Lizzie on your hands,' says Dan, who held the girl in his arms.

"'What do you mean?' Sam inquired.

"'She's on my hands an' she's goin' to stay there,' says the young man. 'I'm in love with Lizzie myself. I've always been in love with Lizzie.'

"'Your confession is ill-timed,' says Lizzie, as she pulled away an' tried to smooth her hair. She began to cry

again, an' added, between sobs: 'My
heart is about broken, and I must
go home and get help for my poor
father.'

"'I'll attend to that,' says Dan;
'but I warn you that I'm goin' to
offer a Pettigrew for a Henshaw even.
If I had a million dollars I'd give it
all to boot.'

"Sam turned toward me, his face
red as a beet.

"'The money!' he shouted. 'Get it,
quick!'

"'Here it is!' I said, as I put the
roll o' bills in his hand.

"'Did you take it off him?'

"'I took it off him.'

"'Poor Aleck!' he says, mournfully,
as he counted the money. 'It's kind
o' hard on him.'

"Soon we halted a passin' automobile an' got Sam up the bank an' over

the wall. It was like movin' a piano
with somebody playin' on it, but we
managed to seat him on the front
floor o' the car, which took us all
home.

"So the affair ended without dis-
grace to any one, if not without violence, and no one knows of the cablegram save the few persons directly
concerned. But the price of Alecks
took a big slump in Pointview. No
han'some foreign gent could marry
any one in this village, unless it was
a chambermaid in a hotel.

"That was the end of the first heat
of the race with Lizzie in Pointview.
Aleck had folded up his bluff an'
silently sneaked away. I heard no
more of him save from a lady with
blond, curly hair an' a face done in
water-colors, who called at my office
one day to ask about him, an' who

proved to my satisfaction that she was his wife, an' who remarked with real, patrician accent when I told her the truth about him: 'Ah, g'wan, yer kiddin' me.'

"I began to explore the mind of Lizzie, an' she acted as my guide in the matter. For her troubles the girl was about equally indebted to her parents an' the Smythe school. Now the Smythe school had been founded by the Reverend Hopkins Smythe, an Englishman who for years had been pastor of the First Congregational Church — a soothin' man an' a favorite of the rich New-Yorkers. People who hadn't slept for weeks found repose in the First Congregational Church an' Sanitarium of Pointview. They slept an' snored while the Reverend Hopkins wept an' roared. His rhetoric was better than

bromide or sulphonal. In grateful rec-
ollection of their slumbers, they set
him up in business.

"Now I'm agoin' to talk as mean
as I feel. Sometimes I get tired o'
bein' a gentleman an' knock off for
a season o' rest an' refreshment.
Here goes! The school has some
good girls in it, but most of 'em
are indolent candy-eaters. Their life
is one long, sweet dream broken
by nightmares of indigestion. Their
study is mainly a bluff; their books
a merry jest; their teachers a butt of
ridicule. They're the veriest little
pagans. Their religion is, in fact, a
kind of Smythology. Its High Priest
is the Reverend Hopkins. Its Jupi-
ter is self. Its lesser gods are princes,
dukes, earls, counts, an' barons. Its
angels are actors an' tenors. Its bap-
tism is flattery. Poverty an' work

are its twin hells. Matrimony is its heaven, an' a slippery place it is. They revel in the best sellers an' the worst smellers. They gossip of intrigue an' scandal. They get their lessons if they have time. They cheat in their examinations. If the teacher objects she is promptly an' generally insulted. She has to submit or go— for the girls stand together. It's a sort of school-girls' union. They'd quit in a body if their fun were seriously interrupted, an' Mr. Smythe couldn't afford that, you know. He wouldn't admit it, but they've got him buffaloed.

"Lizzie no sooner got through than she set out with her mother to find the prince. She struck Aleck in Italy."

Socrates leaned back and laughed.

"Now, if you please, I'll climb back on my pedestal," he said.

"Thank God! Lizzie began to rise above her education. She went to work in her father's store, an' the whole gang o' Lizzie-chasers had to change their gait again. She organized our prosperous young ladies' club—a model of its kind—the purpose of which is the promotion of simple livin' an' a taste for useful work. They have fairs in the churches, an' I distribute a hundred dollars in cash prizes—five dollars each for the best exhibits o' pumpkin-pie, chicken-pie, bread, rolls, coffee, roast turkey, plain an' fancy sewin', an' so on. One by one the girls are takin' hold with us an' lettin' go o' the grand life. They've begun to take hold o' the broom an' the dish-cloth, an' the boys seem to be takin' hold o' them with more vigor an' determination. The boys are concluding that it's cheaper to buy a piano-player than to marry one, that canned prima-donnas are better than the home-grown article, that women are more to be desired than playthings.

IV

IN WHICH THE HAM WAR HAS ITS
BEGINNING

"ONE day in the old time a couple of industrious Yankees were hard at work in a field," Socrates continued. "Suddenly one said to the other:

"'I wish I was worth ten thousand dollars.'

"An' the other asked:

"'What would ye do with it?'

"The wisher rested on his shovel an' gave his friend a look of utter contempt.

"'What would I do with it?' he said. 'Why, you cussed fool, I'd set down—an' without blamin' myself.'

74

"By-and-by the Yankee got to set-tin' down without blamin' himself, an' also without the ten thousand. Here in Pointview we're learnin' how to stand up again, an' Lizzie is responsible. You shall hear how it happened.

"First I must tell you that Dan had been makin' little progress in the wooin' o' Lizzie. Now she was inclined to go slow. Lizzie was fond o' Dan. She put on her best clothes when he came to see her of a Sunday. She sang to him, she walked him about the place with her arm in his, but she tenderly refused to agree to marry him. When he grew sentimental she took him out among the cucumbers in the garden. She permitted no sudden rise in his temperature.

"'I will not marry,' she said, 'until I have done what I can to repay my

75

father for all that he has tried to do for me. I must be uneducated and re-educated. It may take a long time. Meanwhile you may meet some one you like better. I'm not going to pledge you to wait for me. Of course I shall be awfully proud and pleased if you do wait, but, Dan, I want you to be free. Let's both be free until we're ready.'

"It was bully. Dan pleaded with the eloquence of an old-fashioned lawyer. Lizzie stood firm behind this high fence, an' she was right. With Dan in debt an' babies comin', what could she have done for her father? Suddenly it seemed as if all the young men had begun to take an interest in Lizzie, an', to tell the truth, she was about the neatest, sweetest little myrmidon of commerce that ever wore a white apron. The light of

true womanhood had begun to shine
in her face. She kept the store in
apple-pie order, an' everybody was
well treated. The business grew. Sam
bought a small farm outside the village with crops in, an' moved there
for the summer. Soon he began to
let down his prices. The combine
was broken. It was the thing we
had been waitin' for. People flocked
to his store. The others came down,
but too late. Sam held his gain, an'
Lizzie was the power behind the fat.
Dan finished his course in agriculture
an' I bought him a farm, an' he went
to work there, but he spent half his
time in the store of his father tryin'
to keep up with Lizzie. Suddenly
Dan started a ham war. He cut the
price of hams five cents a pound.
Ham was one of our great staples, an'
excitement ran high. Lizzie cut be-

low him two cents a pound. Dan
cut the price again. Lizzie made
no effort to meet this competition.
The price had gone below the wholesale rate by quite a margin. People
thronged to Dan's emporium. Wom-
en stood on the battle-field, their necks
blanched with powder, their cheeks
bearin' the red badge o' courage, an'
every man you met had a ham in his
hand. The Pettigrew wagon hurried
hither an' thither loaded with hams.
Even the best friends of Sam an'
Lizzie were seen in Dan's store buyin'
hams. They laid in a stock for all
winter. Suddenly Dan quit an' re-
stored his price to the old figure.
Lizzie continued to sell at the same
price, an' was just as cheerful as ever.
She had won the fight, an' ye wouldn't
think that anything unusual had happened; but wait an' see.

"Every day boys an' girls were droppin' out o' the clouds an' goin' to work tryin' to keep up with Lizzie. The hammocks swung limp in the breeze. The candy stores were almost deserted, an' those that sat by the fountains were few. We were learnin' how to stand up.

"One day Dan came into my office all out o' gear. He looked sore an' discouraged. I didn't wonder.

"'What's the matter now?' I says.

"'I don't believe Lizzie cares for me.'

"'How's that?' I says.

"'Last Sunday she was out riding with Tom Bryson, an' every Sunday afternoon I find half-a-dozen young fellows up there.'

"'Well, ye know, Lizzie is attractive, an' she ain't our'n yit—not just yit,' I says. 'If young men come to see her she's got to be polite to 'em. You wouldn't expect her to take a broom an' shoo 'em off?'

"'But I don't have anything to do with other girls.'

"'An' you're jealous as a hornet,' I says. 'Lizzie wants you to meet other girls. When Lizzie marries it will be for life. She'll want to know that you love her an' only her. You keep right on tryin' to catch up with Lizzie, an' don't be worried.'

"He stopped strappin' the razor of his discontent, but left me with unhappy looks. That very week I saw him ridin' about with Marie Benson in his father's motor-car.

"Soon a beautiful thing happened. I have told you of the melancholy end of the cashier of one of our local banks. Well, in time his wife followed him to the cemetery. She was

a distant relative of Sam's wife an'
a friend of Lizzie. We found easy
employment for the older children,
an' Lizzie induced her parents to
adopt two that were just out of their
mother's arms—a girl of one an' a
boy of three years. I suggested to
Lizzie that it seemed to me a serious
undertaking, but she felt that she
ought to be awfully good by way of
atonement for the folly of her past
life. It was near the end of the year,
an' I happen to know that when
Christmas came a little sack contain-
ing five hundred dollars in gold was
delivered at Sam Henshaw's door for
Lizzie from a source unknown to her.
That paid for the nurse, an' eased the
situation."

V

IN WHICH LIZZIE EXERTS AN INFLU-
ENCE ON THE AFFAIRS OF THE
RICH AND GREAT

A YEAR after Socrates Potter had told of the descent of Lizzie, and the successful beginning of her new life, I called again at his office.

"How is Pointview?" I asked.

"Did ye ever learn how it happened to be called Pointview?" he inquired.

"No."

"Well, it began with a little tavern with a tap-room called the Pointview House, a great many years ago. Travellers used to stop an' look around for the Point, an', of course, they couldn't see it, for there's none here; at least, no point of land. They'd go in an' order drinks an' say:

"'Landlord, where's the point?'

"An' the landlord would say: 'Well, boys, if you ain't in a hurry you'll probably see it purty soon.'

"All at once it would appear to 'em, an' it was apt to be an' amusin' bit o' scenery.

"We've always been quick to see a point here, an' anxious to show it to other people."

He leaned back and laughed as one foot sought the top of his desk.

"Our balloons rise from every walk o' life an' come down out o' ballast," he went on. "Many of 'em touch ground in the great financial aviation park that surrounds Wall Street. In our stages of recovery the power of Lizzie has been widely felt."

Up went his other foot. I saw that the historical mood was upon him.

"Talk about tryin' to cross the Atlantic in an air-ship—why, that's conservative," he continued. "Right here in the eastern part o' Connecticut lives a man who set out for the vicinity of the moon with a large company—a joint-stock company—in his life-boat. First he made the journey with the hot-air-ship of his mind, an' came back with millions in the hold of his imagination. Then he thought he'd experiment with a corporation of his friends—his surplus friends. They got in on the ground floor, an' got out in the sky. Most of 'em were thrown over for ballast. The Wellman of this enterprise escaped with his life an' a little wreckage. He was Mr. Thomas Robinson

84

Barrow, an' he came to consult me about his affairs. They were in bad shape.

"'Sell your big house an' your motor-cars,' I urged.

"'That would have been easy,' he answered, 'but Lizzie has spoilt the market for luxuries. You remember how she got high notions up at the Smythe school, an' began a life of extravagance, an' how we all tried to keep up with her, an' how the rococo architecture broke out like pimples on the face of Connecticut?'

"I smiled an' nodded.

"'Well, it was you, I hear, that helped her back to earth and started her in the simpleton life. Since then she has been going just as fast, but in the opposite direction, and we're still tryin' to keep up with her. Now I found a man who was going to buy my property, but suddenly his wife decided that they would get along with a more modest outfit. She's trying to keep up with Lizzie. Folks are getting wise.'

"'Why don't you?'

"'Can't.'

"'Why not?'

"'Because I'm a born fool. We're fettered; we're prisoners of luxury.'

"Only a night or two before I had seen his wife at a reception with a rope of pearls in her riggin' an' a search-light o' diamonds on her forward deck an' a tiara-boom-de-ay at her masthead an' the flags of opulence flyin' fore an' aft.

"'If I were you,' I said, 'I'd sell everything—even the jewels.'

"'My poor wife!' he exclaimed. 'I haven't the heart to tell her all. She don't know how hard up we are!'

86

"'I wouldn't neglect her education if I were you,' I said. 'There's a kindness, you know, that's most unkind. Some day I shall write an article on the use an' abuse of tiaras —poor things! It isn't fair to overwork the family tiara. I suggest that you get a good-sized trunk an' lock it up with the other jewels for a vacation. If necessary your house could be visited by a burglar—that is, if you wanted to save the feelin's of your wife.'

"He turned with a puzzled look at me.

"'Is it possible that you haven't heard of that trick?' I asked—'a man of your talents!'

"He shook his head.

"'Why, these days, if a man wishes to divorce the family jewels an' is afraid of his wife, the house is always entered by a burglar. My dear sir, the burglar is an ever-present help in time of trouble. It's a pity that we have no *Gentleman's Home Journal* in which poor but deservin' husbands could find encouragement an' inspiration.'

"He looked at me an' laughed.

"'Suppose you engage a trusty and reliable burglar?' he proposed.

"'There's only one in the world,' I said.

"'Who is it?'

"'Thomas Robinson Barrow. Of course, I'm not sayin' that if *I* needed a burglar he's just the man I should choose, but for this job he's the only reliable burglar. Try him.'

"He seemed to be highly amused.

"'But it might be difficult to fool the police,' he said, in a minute.

"'Well, it isn't absolutely necessary, you know,' I suggested. 'The Chief of Police is a friend of mine.'

"'Good! I'm engaged for this job, and will sell the jewels and turn the money over to you.'

"'I do not advise that—not just that,' I said. 'We'll retire them from active life. A tiara in the safe is worth two in the Titian bush. We'll use them for collateral an' go to doin' business. When we've paid the debts in full we'll redeem the goods an' return them to your overjoyed wife. We'll launch our tiara on the Marcel waves.'

"Tom was delighted with this plan —not the best, perhaps—but, anyhow, it would save his wife from reproach, an' I don't know what would have happened if she had continued to dazzle an' enrage his creditors with the pearls an' the tiara.

"'It will not be so easy to sell the house,' Tom went on. 'That's our worst millstone. It was built for large hospitality, and we have a good many friends, and they come every week and jump on to the millstone.'

"'If one has to have a millstone he should choose it with discretion,' I said. 'It doesn't pay to get one that is too inviting. You'll have to swim around with yours for a while, and watch your chance to slip it on to some other fellow's neck. You don't want your son to be a millstonaire. Some day a man of millions may find it a comfortable fit, an' relieve you. They're buyin' places all about here.'

"Tom left an' began work on our programme. The burglary was well executed an' advertised. It achieved a fair amount of publicity—not too much, you know, but enough. The

place was photographed by the re-
porters with the placard 'For Sale'
showin' plainly on the front lawn.
The advertisin' was worth almost as
much as the diamonds. Tom said
that his wife had lost weight since
the sad event.

"'Of course,' I said. 'You can't
take ten pounds of jewelry from a
woman without reducin' her weight.
She must have had a pint o' diamonds.'

"Pictures an' glowin' accounts of
the villa were printed in all the
papers, an' soon a millionaire wrote
that it was just the place he was
lookin' for. I closed the deal with
him. It was Bill Warburton, who
used to go to school with me up there
on the hills. He had long been
dreamin' of a home in Pointview.

"They used to say that Bill was a

fool, but he proved an alibi. Went West years ago an' made a fortune, an' thought it would be nice to come back an' finish his life where it began, near the greatest American city. I drew the papers, an' Bill an' I got together often an' talked of the old happy days, now glimmering in the far past—some thirty-five years away.

"Well, they enlarged the house— that was already big enough for a hotel—an' built stables an' kennels an' pheasant yards an' houses for ducks an' geese an' peacocks. They stocked up with fourteen horses, twelve hounds, nine collies, four setters, nineteen servants, innumerable fowls, an' four motor-cars, an' started in pursuit o' happiness.

"You see, they had no children, an' all these beasts an' birds were intended to supply the deficiency in

BILL AN' I GOT TOGETHER OFTEN AN' TALKED OF THE OLD HAPPY DAYS

human life, an' assist in the campaign. Well, somehow, it didn't succeed, an' one day Bill came into my office with a worried look. He confided to me the well-known fact that his wife was nervous and unhappy.

"'The doctors don't do her any good, an' I thought I'd try a lawyer,' said he.

"'Do you want to sue Fate for damages or indict her for malicious persecution?' I asked.

"'Neither,' he said, 'but you know the laws of nature as well as the laws of men. I appeal to you to tell me what law my wife has broken, and how she can make amends.'

"'You surprise me,' I said. 'You an' the madame can have everything you want, an' still you're unhappy.'

"'What can we have that you can't? You can eat as much, an'

93

sleep better, an' wear as many clothes, an' see an' hear as well as we can.'

"'Ah, but in the matter of quality I'm way behind the flag, Bill. You can wear cloth o' gold, an Russian sables, an' have champagne an' terrapin every meal, an' fiddlers to play while ye eat it, an' a brass band to march around the place with ye, an' splendid horses to ride, an' dogs to roar on ahead an' attract the attention of the populace. You can have a lot of bankrupt noblemen to rub an' manicure an' adulate an' chiropodize ye, an' people who'd have to laugh at your wit or look for another job, an' authors to read from their own works—'

"Bill interrupted with a gentle protest: 'Soc, how comforting you are!'

"'Well, if all that is losin' its charm, what's the matter with travel?'

"'Don't talk to me about travel,' said Bill. 'We've worn ruts in the earth now. Our feet have touched every land.'

"'How many meals do you eat a day?'

"'Three.'

"'Try six,' I suggested.

"He laughed, an' I thought I was makin' progress, so I kept on.

"'How many motor-cars have ye?'

"'Four.'

"'Get eight,' I advised, as Bill put on the loud pedal. 'You've got nineteen servants, I believe, try thirty-eight. You have—twenty-one dogs —get forty-two. You can afford it.'

"'Come, be serious,' said Bill. 'Don't poke fun at me.'

"'Ah! but your wife must be able to prove that she has more dogs an' horses an' servants an' motor-cars,

7

an' that she eats more meals in a day than any other woman in Connecticut. Then, maybe, she'll be happy. You know it's a woman's ambition to excel.'

"'We have too many fool things now,' said Bill, mournfully. 'She's had enough of them—God knows!'

"Something in Bill's manner made me sit up and stare at him.

"'Of course, you don't mean that she wants another husband!' I exclaimed.

"'I'm not so sure of that,' said Bill, sadly. 'Sometimes I'm almost inclined to think she does.'

"'Well, that's one direction in which I should advise strict economy,' said I. 'You can multiply the dogs an' the horses, an' the servants an' the motor-cars, but in the matter o' wives an' husbands we ought to stick

to the simple life. Don't let her go
to competing with those Fifth Avenue
ladies.'

"'I don't know what's the matter,'
Bill went on. 'She's had everything
that her heart could wish. But, of
course, she has had only one husband,
and most of her friends have had
two or three. They've outmarried
her. It may be that, secretly, she's
just a little annoyed about that.
Many of her old friends are consumed
with envy; their bones are rotten
with it. They smile upon her; they
accept her hospitality; they declare
their love, and they long for her
downfall. Now, my wife has a certain pride and joy in all this, but,
naturally, it breeds a sense of loneliness—the bitter loneliness that one
may find only in a crowd. She turns
more and more to me, and, between

ourselves, she seems to have made up her mind that I don't love her, and I can't convince her that I do.'

"'Well, Bill, I should guess that you have always been fond of your wife—and—true to her.'

"'And you are right,' said Bill. 'I've loved with all my heart and with a conscience. It's my only pride, for, of course, I might have been gay. In society I enjoy a reputation for firmness. It is no idle boast.'

"'Well, Bill, you can't do anything more for her in the matter of food, raiment, beasts, or birds, an' as to jewelry she carries a pretty heavy stock. I often feel the need of smoked glasses when I look at her. You'll have to make up your mind as to whether she needs more or less. I'll study the situation myself. It

may be that I can suggest something
by - and - by — just as a matter of
friendship.'

"'Your common sense may dis-
cern what is needed,' said Bill. 'I
wish you'd come at least once a week
to dinner. My wife would be delighted to have you, Soc. You are
one of the few men who interest
her.'

"She was a pretty woman, distinguished for a look of weariness and
a mortal fear of fat. She had done
nothing so hard an' so long, that, to
her, nothing was all there was in the
world—save fat. She was so busy
about it that she couldn't sit still an'
rest. She wandered from one chair
to another, smokin' a cigarette, an'
now and then glancin' at her image
in a mirror an' slyly feelin' her ribs
to see if she had gained flesh that day.

99

She liked me because I was unlike any other man she had met. I poked fun at her folly an' all the grandeur of the place. I amused her as much as she amused me, perhaps. Anyhow, we got to be good friends, an' the next Sunday we all drove out in a motor - car to see Lizzie. Mrs. Bill wanted to meet her. Lizzie had become famous. She was walkin' up an' down the lawn with the infant in a perambulator, an' the small boy toddling along behind her. We left Mrs. Bill with Lizzie an' the kids, an' set out for a tramp over the big farm. When we returned we found the ladies talkin' earnestly in the house.

"Before we left I called Lizzie aside for a minute.

"'How do you get along with these babies?' I asked.

"'They're the life of our home.

WE SET OUT FOR A TRAMP OVER THE BIG FARM

My father and mother think they couldn't live without them.'

"'An' they're good practice for you,' I suggested. 'It's time you were plannin' for yourself, Lizzie.'

"'I've no prospects,' said she.

"'How is that?'

"'Why, there's only one boy that I care for, an' he has had enough of me.'

"'You don't mean Dan?'

"'Yes,' she whispered with trembling lips, an' turned away.

"'What's the matter?'

"She pulled herself together an' answered in half a moment: 'Oh, I don't know! He doesn't come often. He goes around with other girls.'

"'Well,' I said, 'it's the same ol' story. He's only tryin' to keep up with Lizzie. You've done some goin' around yourself.'

"'I know, but I couldn't help it.'

"'He knows, an' he couldn't help it,' I says. 'The boys have flocked around you, an' the girls have flocked around Dan. They were afraid he'd get lonesome. If I were you I'd put a mortgage on him an' foreclose it as soon as possible.'

"'It's too late,' says she. 'I hear he's mortgaged.'

"'You'd better search the records,' I says, 'an' if it ain't so, stop bein' careless. You've put yer father on his feet. Now look out for yerself.'

"'I think he's angry on account of the ham war,' says she.

"'Why do you think that?'

"She told me the facts, an' I laughed 'til the tears came to my eyes.

"'Nonsense,' I says, 'Dan will like that. You wait 'til I tell him, an'

102

he'll be up here with his throttle wide open.'

"'Do you suppose he'd spend Christmas with us?' she asked, with a very sober look. 'You know, his mother an' father have gone South, an' he'll be all alone.'

"'Ask him at once—call him on the 'phone,' I advised, an' bade her good-bye.

"The happiness o' Lizzie an' the charm o' those kids had suggested an idea. I made up my mind that I'd try to put Mr. an' Mrs. Bill on the job o' keepin' up with Lizzie.

"'That's a wonderful woman,' said Mrs. Bill, as we drove away. 'I envy her—she's so strong and well and happy. She loves those babies, and is in the saddle every afternoon, helping with the work o' the farm.'

"'Why don't you get into the saddle and be as well and strong as she is?' Bill asked.

"'Because I've no object—it's only a way of doing nothing,' said Mrs. Bill. 'I'm weary of riding for exercise. There never was a human being who could keep it up long. It's like you and your dumb-bells. To my knowledge you haven't set a foot in your gymnasium for a month. As a matter of fact, you're as tired of play as I am, every bit. Why don't you go into Wall Street an' get poor?'

"'Tired of play!' Bill exclaimed. 'Why, Grace, night before last you were playing bridge until three o'clock in the morning.'

"'Well, it's a way of doing nothing skilfully and on the competitive plan,' said she. 'It gives me a chance to measure my capacity. When I get through I am so weary that often I can go to sleep without thinking. It seems to me that brains are a great nuisance to one who has no need of them. Of course, by-and-by, they'll atrophy and disappear like the tails of our ancestors. Meanwhile, I suppose they are bound to get sore. Mine is such a fierce, ill-bred, impudent sort of a brain, and it's as busy as a bat in a belfry. I often wish that I had one of those soft, flexible, paralytic, cocker-spaniel brains, like that of our friend Mrs. Seavey. She is so happy with it — so unterrified. She is equally at home in bed or on horseback, reading the last best seller or pouring tea and compliments. Now just hear how this brain of mine is going on about that poor, inoffensive creature! But that's the way it treats me. It's a perfect heathen of a brain.'

"Bill an' I looked at each other an' laughed. Her talk convinced me of one thing—that her trouble was not the lack of a brain.

"'You're always making fun of me,' she said. 'Why don't you give me something to do?'

"'Suppose you wash the dishes?' said Bill.

"'Would it please you?'

"'Anything that pleases you pleases me.'

"I saw that she, too, was goin' to try to keep up with Lizzie, an' I decided that I'd help her. When we arrived at the villa we made our way to its front door through a pack of collie dogs out for an airing.

"'By - the - way,' I said, when we sat down to luncheon at Bill's house, 'congratulate me. I'm a candidate for new honors.'

"I'M A CANDIDATE FOR NEW HONORS"

"'Those of a husband? I've been hoping for that—you stubborn old bachelor,' said Mrs. Bill, expectantly.

"'No,' I answered, 'I'm to be a father.'

"Bill put down his fork an' turned an' stared at me. Mrs. Bill leaned back in her chair with a red look of surprise.

"'The gladdest, happiest papa in Connecticut,' I added.

"Mrs. Bill covered her face with her napkin an' began to shake.

"'S-Soc., have you fallen?' Bill stammered.

"'No, I've riz,' I said. 'Don't blame me, ol' man, I had to do it. I've adopted some orphans. I'm goin' to have an orphanage on the hill; but it will take a year to finish it. I'm goin' to have five children. They're beauties, an' I know that I'm goin' to love them. I propose to take them out of the atmosphere of indigence an' wholesale charity. They'll have a normal, pleasant home, an' a hired mother an' me to look after them —the personal touch, you know. I expect to have a lot of fun with them.'

"'But what a responsibility!' said Mrs. Bill.

"'I know, but I feel the need of it. Of course it's different with you— very different—you have all these dogs an' horses to be responsible for an' to give you amusement. I couldn't afford that. Then, too, I'm a little odd, I guess. I can get more fun out of one happy, human soul than out of all the dogs an' horses in creation.'

"'But children! Why, they're so subject to sickness and accident and death,' said Mrs. Bill.

"'An' they're subject, also, to health an' life an' safety,' I answered.

"'Yes, but you know—they'll be getting into all kinds of trouble. They'll worry you.'

"'True; but as for worry, I don't mind that much,' I said. 'My best days were those that were full of worry. Now, that I've won a competence an' my worries are gone, so is half my happiness. You can't have sunshine without shadows. There was one of my neighbors who was troubled with "boils." He had to have 'em cured right away, an' a doctor gave him some medicine that healed 'em up, but he was worse off than ever. The boils began to do business inside of him, an' he rushed back to the doctor.

"'"What's the matter now?" said the medical man.

"'"Outside I'm sound as a dollar," said my neighbor, "but it seems as if all hell had moved into me."

"'Now, cares are like boils: it don't do to get rid of 'em too quick. They're often a great relief to the inside of a man, an' it's better to have 'em on the surface than way down in your marrow.'

"Bill an' his wife looked into each other's eyes for half a minute, but neither spoke.

"'I'm goin' to ask a favor of you,' I said. 'I see that there's nobody livin' in the old farm-house out back of the garden. I wish you'd let me put my little family into it until I can build a home for 'em.'

"'Oh, my!' Mrs. Bill exclaimed. 'Those children would be running all over the lawns and the garden. They'd destroy my roses.'

"'True; but, after all, they're more beautiful than the roses,' I urged. 'They're more graceful in form, more charming in color. Then, too, roses cannot laugh or weep or play. Roses cannot look up at you out of eyes full of the light of heaven an' brighter than your jewels. Roses may delight, but they cannot love you or know that you love them. Dear woman, my roses will wander over the lawns. Their colors will be flickering about you, and the music of their voices will surround the villa some days; but, God knows, they'll look better, far better than the dogs or the bronze lions, or the roses. I shall dress them well.'

"'I think he's right,' said Bill.

"'He's most disturbing and persuasive anyway—the revolutionist!' said Mrs. Bill. 'If it's really a favor

8

to you, Mr. Potter, I shall agree to
it. But you must have a trusty
woman. I really cannot assume any
responsibility.'

"I thanked her and promised to
assume all responsibility, and Mrs.
Warburton was to get the old house
ready at once.

"Three days later I drove to the
villa with my matron and the babies.
Rather quick work, wasn't it? I
hadn't let any grass grow under my
plan. When we lit at the front door
every youngster broke out in a loud
hurrah of merriment. The three-
year-old boy—beautiful beyond all
words—got aboard one of the crouch-
ed lions and began to shout. A little
girl made a grab at the morning-
glories on a Doric column, while her
sister had mounted a swinging seat
an' tumbled to the floor. The other

THREE DAYS LATER I DROVE TO THE VILLA

two were chattering like parrots. Honestly, I was scared. I was afraid that Mrs. Bill would come down and jump into hysterics. I snaked the boy off the lion's back and rapped on him for order. The matron got busy with the others. In a jiffy it seemed as if they had all begun to wail an' roar. I trembled when a maid open- ed the door an' I saw Mrs. Bill comin' down the staircase. I wouldn't have been surprised to have seen the bronze lion get up an' run.

"'The saints defend us!' exclaimed Mrs. Bill, in the midst of the uproar.

"'They're not at their best,' I shouted, 'but here they are.'

"'Yes, I knew they were there,' said Mrs. Bill. 'This is the music of which you were speaking the other day. Take them right around to the old house, if you please. I'm sorry, but I must ask you to excuse me this morning.'

"I succeeded in quellin' the tumult, and introduced the matron, who received a nod an' a look that made a dent in her, an' away we went around the great house, a melancholy, shuffling troop, now silent as the grave. It looked dark for my little battalion with which I had been hoping to conquer this world within the villa gates. They were of the great army of the friendless.

"I asked Mrs. Hammond, the matron, to see that they did as little damage as possible, and left them surrounded by every comfort.

"They had a telephone and unlimited credit at the stores, an' Mrs. Hammond was a motherly soul of much experience with children, an' I knew that I could trust her.

THE BOY EXERTED HIS CHARMS UPON
MY LADY WARBURTON

"I was to dine with the Warbur-
tons later in the week, an' before I
entered the big house that evening
I went around to the lodge. The
children were all well an' asleep in
their beds, an' the matron apparently
happy an' contented. She said that
Mrs. Bill had met them in the grounds
that day, an' she told how the little three-year-old boy had exerted his
charms upon my lady Warburton,
who had spent half an hour leading
him through the gardens.

"How beautiful he was lying asleep
in his bed that evening!—his face
like the old dreams of Eros, with
silken, yellow, curly locks on his brow,
an' long dark lashes, soft as the silk
of the growing corn, an' a red mouth,
so wonderfully curved, so appealing
in its silence. Beneath it were teeth
like carved ivory. Those baby lips

seemed to speak to me and to say: 'O man that was born of a woman, and like me was helpless, give me your love or look not upon me!'

"But I could not help looking, an' as I looked he smiled in what dreams —of things past or to come—I wish it were in me to tell you. Something touched me—like a strong hand. I went out under the trees in the darkness an' stood still an' wondered what had happened to me. Great Scott! —me! Socrates Potter, lawyer, statesman, horse-trader!

"'With that little captain I could take a city,' I whispered, an' I got up an' brushed myself off, as it were, an' walked around to the front door of the great house.

"Therein I was to witness an amusing comedy. The butler wore a new sort of grin as he took my wraps at the door. There were guests, mostly from New York an' Green-wich. We had taken our seats at the table when, to my surprise, Mrs. Bill, in a grand costume, with a tiara on her head, an' a collar of diamonds on her neck, began to serve the caviar.

"'Ladies and gentlemen,' said she, 'this is to convince Mr. Socrates Potter that I can do useful work. I'm dieting, anyhow, and I can't eat.'

"'My friend, I observe that you are serving us, and we are proud, but you do not appear to be serving a pur-pose,' I said.

"'Now, don't spoil it all with your relentless logic,' she began. 'You see, I am going to take a hand in this keeping-up-with-Lizzie business. One of our ladies had to give up a dinner-party the other day, because her but-lers had left suddenly.'

"""Why didn't you and a maid serve the dinner yourselves?" I said.

"""Impossible!" was her proud answer.

"""It would have been a fine lark. I would have done it," I said.

"""I'd like to see you," she laughed.

"""You shall," I answered, and here I am.'

"Now, there were certain smiles which led me to suspect that it was a blow aimed at one of the ladies who sat at the table with us, but of that I am not sure.

"'I'm also getting my hand in,' our hostess went on. 'Bill and I are going to try the simple life. To-morrow we move into the log-cabin, where we shall do our own work, and send the servants off for a week's holiday. I'm going to do the cooking—I've been learning how—and I shall make the beds, and Bill is to chop the wood, and help wash the dishes, and we shall sleep out-of-doors. It will, I hope, be a lesson to some of these proud people around us who are living beyond their means. That's good, isn't it?'

"'Excellent!' I exclaimed, as the others laughed.

"'Incidentally, it will help me to reduce,' she added.

"'An' it promises to reduce Bill,' I said. 'It will kill Bill, I fear, but it will pay. You might change your plan a little—just a little—an' save poor Bill. Think of eating biscuit an' flapjacks from the hand of a social leader! Between the millstones of duty and indigestion he will be sadly ground, but with the axe he may, if he will, defend his constitution.'

"'Well, what's a constitution between husband and wife?' she asked.

"'Nothin',' I says. 'Bear in mind I wouldn't discourage you. With the aid of the axe his ancestors were able to withstand the assaults of pork an' beans an' pie. If he uses it freely, he is safe.'

"'You see, I shall have him in a position where he must work or die,' said Mrs. Bill.

"'He'll die,' said a guest.

"'I call it a worthy enterprise whatever the expense,' I said. 'It will set a fashion here an' a very good one. In this community there are so many dear ladies who are prisoners of gravitation. They rely almost exclusively on hired hands an' feet, an' are losin' the use o' their own. What confusion will spread among them when they learn that Mrs. William Henry

Warburton, the richest woman in Fairfield County, and the daughter of a bishop, has been doin' her own work! What consternation! What dismay! What female profanity! What a revision of habits an' resolutions! Why, there's been nothin' like it since the descent of Lizzie.'

"'I think it's terrible,' said a fat lady from Louisville, distinguished for her appetite, an' often surreptitiously referred to as 'The Mammoth Cave of Kentucky.' 'The idea of trying to make it fashionable to endure drudgery! I think we women have all we can do now.'

"'To be respectable,' said Mrs. Bill; 'but let's try to do something else.'

"'Why don't you form a Ladies' Protective Union,' Bill suggested, 'an' choose the tiara for a symbol, an' strike for no hours a day an' all your husbands can earn?'

"'And the employment of skilled idlers only,' Mrs. Bill put in. 'They must all know how to do nothing in the modern way—by discussing the rights of women and the novel of lust, and the divorces past and prospective, by playing at bridge and benevolence. How absurd it all is! I'm not going to be an overgrown child any longer.'

"I saw that Mrs. Bill was makin' progress, an' with her assistance I began to hope for better things in that neighborhood.

"You've got to reach the women somehow, you see, before you can improve the social conditions of a community. I love them, but many are overgrown children, as Mrs. Bill had put it, an' doin' nothing with

singular skill an' determination an'
often with appalling energy.

"Our pretty hostess had been helping a butler, as this talk went on,
an' presently one of the other ladies
joined her, an' never was any company so picturesquely an' amusingly
served.

"'I've quite fallen in love with that
three-year-old boy,' said Mrs. Bill,
as we rose from the table. 'I had a
good romp with him to-day.'

"'I wish you'd go over to the old
farm-house with me; I want to show
you something,' I said.

"In a moment we were in wraps
an' making our way across the
lawn.

"'I was glad to get a rap at that
Mrs. Barrow,' she whispered, as we
walked along. 'She's just got back
her jewels that were stolen, and has

begun to go out again. She's the vainest, proudest fool of a woman, and her husband is always borrowing money. Did you know it?'

"'Some—that is, fairly well,' I said, with bitterness.

"'So does Bill, and she goes about with the airs of a grand lady and the silliest notions. Really, it was for her benefit that I helped the butler.'

"'If it weren't for Bill I'd call you an angel,' I said. 'You have it in your power to redeem the skilled idlers of this community.'

"We reached the little house so unlike the big, baronial thing we had left. It was a home. Mrs. Hammond sat by the reading-lamp in its cozy sitting-room before an open fire. She led us into the bedroom with the lamp in her hand. There lay the boy as I had left him, still smiling

SHE LED US INTO THE BEDROOM

with a lovelier, softer red in his cheeks than that of roses.

"'See the color and the dimples,' I said.

"She looked from one to another, an' suddenly the strong appeal of their faces fell upon her. She raised the boy from his bed, an' he put his arms around her neck an' began to talk in a tender baby treble.

"Did you ever hear the voice of a child just out of dreamland, when it expresses, not complaint, but love an' contentment? Well, sir, it is the sweetest, the most compelling note in all nature, I believe. It is like a muted violin—voice of God or voice of man—which is it? I dare not say, but I do know that the song of the hermit-thrush is but sounding brass compared with that.

"I felt its power, an' I said to myself: 'I will waste my life no longer. I will marry.'

"She, too, had felt it. The little captain had almost overcome her. She laid him down, an' we turned away.

"We walked through the garden paths, an' neither spoke, but in the stillness I could hear trumpets of victory. We entered the great hall an' sat with the others by its fireside, but took little part in the talk. When I made my adieus she shook my hand warmly and said I was very good to them.

"Save for its good example, the log-cabin experiment was not a success. They slept with all the doors and windows open, an' one night a skunk came in an' got under the bed. Mrs. Bill discovered that they had company, an' Bill got up an' lit the lantern, an' followed the clew to its source. He threatened an' argued an' appealed to the skunk's better nature with a doughnut, but the little beast sat unmoved in his corner. The place seemed to suit him.

"Bill got mad an' flung the axe at him. It was a fatal move—fatal to the skunk an' the cabin an' the experiment, an' a blow to the sweetness an' sociological condition of Connecticut.

"They returned to the big house, an' by-an'-by told me of their adventure.

"'Don't be discouraged,' I said. 'You will find skunks in every walk of life, but when you do, always throw down your cards an' quit the game. They can deal from the bottom of the pack. You haven't a ghost of a show with 'em.'

"Being driven out of the cabin, Mrs. Bill gave most of her leisure to the farm-house, where I had spent an hour or more every day.

"Suddenly I saw that a wonderful thing had happened to me. I was in love with those kids, an' they with me. The whole enterprise had been a bluff conceived in the interest of the War- burtons. I hadn't really intended to build a house, but suddenly I got busy with all the mechanics I could hire in Pointview, and the house be- gan to grow like a mushroom.

"Another wonderful thing hap- pened. Mrs. Warburton fell in love with the kids, and they with her. She romped with them on the lawn; she took them out to ride every day; she put them to bed every night; she insisted upon buying their clothes; she bought them a pony an' a little

128

omnibus; she built them a playhouse for their comfort. The whole villa began to revolve around the children. They called her mama an' they called me papa, a sufficiently singular situation.

VI

"DAN had been out of town, an' immediately on his return he came to my office.

"'How's business?' I asked.

"'Well, the ham war was a little hard on us, but we're picking up,' says he. 'They're still selling hams way below a decent price over at Henshaw's. I don't see how they can do it.'

"'I do,' I says.

"'Please explain,' says Dan.

"'Don't you know that Lizzie was buyin' most o' those hams that you sold way below the wholesale price, an' that she's now makin' a good profit on 'em?' I says.

"'Great Scott!' Dan exclaimed, as he sank in a chair.

"'The fact is, Dan, the only way to keep up with that girl is to marry her,' says I. 'Get busy. If you don't somebody else will. Put a mortgage on her an' foreclose it as soon as possible. As a floatin' asset Lizzie is dangerous.'

"Dan picked up his hat an' started for the door.

"'Tell her she must do business or you'll cut the price of Pettigrews,' I suggested.

"'Good idea!' he answered, as he went away.

"Meanwhile Mr. an' Mrs. Bill Warburton were hot on the trail of Lizzie.

"Bill came to me one day an' said:

131

'Those babies have solved the problem; my wife is happy and in excellent health. She sleeps an' eats as well as ever, an' her face has a new look—you have observed it?'

"'Certainly, Bill, an' you're goin' to hear some rather chesty an' superior talk. I saw what was the matter long ago—she was motor-sick, an' tiara-sick, an' dog-sick, an' horse-sick. She was sick of idleness an' rich food an' adulation. She has discovered that there are only three real luxuries—work, children, motherhood —that to shirk responsibility is to forfeit happiness. I have been a little disappointed in you, Bill. Your father was a minister; he had the love of men in his soul. You seem to have taken to dogs an' horses with an affection almost brotherly. I don't blame you so much. When men get

rich they naturally achieve a passion
for the things that money will buy.
They think they've got to improve
the breed o' dogs an' horses, an'
they're apt to forget the breed o'
men. You've been pursuin' Happiness with dogs, horses, an' motor-cars.
You never can catch her in that way
—never. Don't you remember, Bill,
that in the old days we didn't pur-
sue Happiness? Why, Happiness pur-
sued us an' generally caught us. Some
days she didn't succeed until we were
all tired out, an' then she led us away
into the wonderful land o' dreams, an'
it was like heaven. You never get
Happiness by pursuin' *her*—that's
one dead sure thing. Happiness is
never captured. She comes unbidden
or not at all. She travels only in one
path, an' you haven't found it. Bill,
we've strayed a little. Let's try to

locate the trail o' Happiness. I believe we're gettin' near it.

"'Last year a colt of yours won a
classic event of the turf. How much
finer it would be if you had some
boys in training for the sublime con-
tests of life, an' it wouldn't cost half
so much. You know, there are plenty
of homeless boys who need your help.
Wouldn't it pay better to develop a
Henry M. Stanley—once a homeless
orphan—than a Salvator or an Or-
monde or a Rayon d'Or?'

"'Pound away,' said Bill. 'Nail
an' rivet me to the cross. I haven't
a word to say, except this: What in
the devil do ye want me to do?'

"'Well, ye might help to redeem
New England,' I said. 'The Yankee
blood is runnin' out, an' it's a pity.
To-day the Yankees are almost a child-
less race. Do ye know the reason?'

"He shook his head.

"'It costs so much to live,' I says. 'We can't afford children. To begin with, the boys an' girls don't marry so young. They can't stand the expense. They're all keepin' up with Lizzie, but on the wrong road. The girls are worse than the boys. They go out o' the private school an' beat the bush for a husband. At first they hope to drive out a duke or an earl; by-an'-by they're willin' to take a common millionaire; at last they conclude that if they can't get a stag they'll take a rabbit. Then we learn that they're engaged to a young man, an' are goin' to marry as soon as he can afford it. He wears himself out in the struggle, an' is apt to be a nervous wreck before the day arrives. They are nearin' or past thirty when he decides that with economy an' *no children* they can afford to maintain a home. The bells ring, the lovely strains from "Lohengrin" fill the grand, new house o' God, an' overflow into the quiet streets o' the village, an' we hear in them what Wagner never thought of — *the joyful death-march of a race*. Think of it, Bill, this old earth is growin' too costly *for the use o' man*. We prefer autos an' diamonds an' knick-knacks! Life has become a kind of a circus where only the favored can pay the price of admission, an' here in America, where about all the great men we have had were bred in cabins, an' everything worth a fish-hook came out o' poverty! You have it in your power to hasten the end o' this wickedness,' I said. 'For one thing, you can make the middleman let go of our throats in this community. Near here are

hundreds of acres o' land goin' to
waste. Buy it an' make it produce
—wool, meat, flax, grains, an' vegetables. Start a market an' a small
factory here, an' satisfy yourself as
to what is a just price for the neces-
saries of life. If the tradesmen are
overchargin' us, they'll have to reduce prices. Put your brain an'
money into it; make it a business.
At least, you'll demonstrate what it
ought to cost to live here in New England. If it's so much that the average Yankee can't afford it by honest
work—if we must all be lawyers or
bankers or brokers or graspin' middle-
men in order to live—let's start a big
Asylum for the Upright, an' give 'em
a chance to die comfortably. But it
isn't so. I can raise potatoes right
here for thirty cents a bushel, as good
as those you pay forty cents a peck

for at Sam Henshaw's. You'll set an example of inestimable value in this republic of ours. Dan has begun the good work, an' demonstrated that it will pay.'

"'It's a good idea—I'm with you,' he said. 'If we can get the boys an' girls to marry while the bloom is on the rye, it's worth while, an' I wouldn't wonder if indirectly we'd increase the crop of Yankees an' the yield of happiness to the acre.'

"'Bill, you're a good fellow,' I said. 'You only need to be reminded of your duty—you're like many another man.'

"'And I'll think you the best fellow in the world if you'll let us keep those kids. We enjoy them. We've been having a lot of fun lately.'

"'I can't do that,' I said, 'but I'll keep 'em here until we can get some

138

more.   There are thousands of them
as beautiful, as friendless, as promising as these were.'

"'I wish you could let us have
these,' he urged.   'We wouldn't adopt
them, probably, but we'd do our best
for them—our very best.'

"'I can't,' I answered.

"'Why?'

"'Because they've got hold of my
old heart—that's why.   I hadn't looked for that, Bill, but the little cusses
have conquered *me*.'

"'Great God!' he exclaimed.   'I
hadn't thought of that.   And my
wife told me this morning that she
loves that three - year - old boy as
dearly as she loves me.   They've
all won her heart.   What shall I
do?'

"'Let me think it over,' I said, an'
shook his hand an' left, an' I knew

139

that I was likely to indulge in the makin' of history right away.

"I went home an' sat down an' wrote the best brief of my career—an appeal to the Supreme Court o' this planet — a woman's heart. It was a letter to one whose name I honored although I had not written it in years.

"Next mornin' I plunged into a lawsuit an' was workin' night an' day, until the jury came in with a verdict an' court adjourned for the Christmas holidays.

"An' that day a decision was handed down in my appeal to the court of last resort. It was a cablegram from an Italian city, an' a verdict in my favor. I am to get in that case the best fee on record—a wife and the love of a dear and beautiful woman. We went to school together,

and I am ashamed that I didn't ask
her to marry me years ago. So much
for me had Lizzie an' the kids accomplished.

"I was to dine with the Warbur-
tons Christmas Eve, and be Santa
Claus for the children. I bought a
set o' whiskers an' put on my big
fur coat and two sets o' bells on the
mare, an' drove to the villa with a
full pack in the buggy an' a fuller
heart in my breast.

"Bill an' Mrs. Bill an' I went over
to the farm-house together with our
arms full. The children were in a
room up-stairs with Mrs. Hammond
waiting for Santa Claus. Below we
helped the two maids, who were trim-
ming the Christmas tree—and a wonderful tree it was when we were done
with it—why, sir, you'd have thought
a rainbow was falling into a thicket

on the edge of a lake. My friend, it was the tree of all fruits.

"We filled the little stockings hanging on the mantel. Then they helped me to put on my beard an' the greatcoat an' cap an' the pack over all, an' Mrs. Bill an' I went out-of-doors. We stood still an' listened for a moment. Two baby voices were calling out of an upper window: 'Santa Claus, please come, Santa Claus!' Then we heard the window close an' the chatter above stairs, but we stood still. Mrs. Bill seemed to be laughing, but I observed that her handkerchief had the centre of the stage in this little comedy.

"In half a minute I stole down the road an' picked up the bells that lay beside it, an' came prancin' to the door with a great jingle, an' in I went an' took my stand by the

THEIR EYES WERE WIDE WITH WONDER

Christmas tree. We could hear the hurry of small feet, an' eager, half-hushed voices in the hall overhead. Then down the stairway came my slender battalion in the last scene of the siege. Their eyes were wide with wonder, their feet slow with fear. The little captain of three years ran straight to Mrs. Bill an' lay hold of her gown, an' partly hid himself in its folds, an' stood peekin' out at me. It was a masterful bit of strategy. I wonder how he could have done it so well. She raised him in her arms an' held him close. A great music-box in a corner began to play:

"'O tannenbaum! O tannenbaum! wie grün
    sind deine blaetter!'

"Then with laughter an' merry jests we emptied the pack, an' gathered from the tree whose fruit has fed

10   143

the starving human heart for more than a thousand years, an' how it filled those friends o' mine!

"Well, it was the night of my life, an' when I turned to go, its climax fell upon me. Mrs. Bill kneeled at my feet, an' said with tears in her eyes, an' her lips an' voice trembling:

"'O Santa Claus! you have given me many things, but I beg for more —five more.'

"The city had fallen. Its queen was on her knees. The victorious army was swarming into the open gate of her arms. The hosts of doubt an' fear were fleeing.

"I refuse to tell you all that happened in the next minute or two. A witness has some rights when testify-in' against his own manhood.

"I helped the woman to her feet, an' said:

144

"'They are yours. I shall be happy enough, and, anyhow, I do not think I shall need them now.'

"An' so I left them as happy as human beings have any right to be. At last they had caught up with Lizzie, an' I, too, was in a fair way to overtake her.

"An' how fared Dan in his pursuit of that remarkable maiden? Why, that very night Lizzie an' Dan had been shakin' the tree o' love, an' I guess the fruit on it was fairly ripe an' meller. Next day they came up to my house together.

"Dan couldn't hold his happiness, an' slopped over as soon as he was inside the door.

"'Mr. Potter,' says he, with more than Christmas merriment, 'we're going to be married next month.'

"Before I could say a word he had

gathered Lizzie up in his arms an'
kissed her, an' she kissed back as
prompt as if it had been a slap in a
game o' tag.

"'You silly man,' she says, 'you
could have had me long ago.'

"'If I'd only 'a' known it,' he says.

"'Oh, the ignorance o' some men!'
she says, lookin' into his eyes.

"'It exceeds the penetration o'
some women,' I says.

"They came together ag'in quite
spiteful. I separated 'em.

"'Quit,' I says. 'Stop pickin' on
each other. It provokes you an' me
too. You're like a pair o' kids turned
loose in a candy store. Behave yer-
selves an' listen to reason.'

"Lizzie turned upon me as if she
thought it was none o' my business.
Then she smiled an' hid her face on
the manly breast o' Dan.

"'Now Lizzie,' I says, 'get yer mind in workin' order as soon as ye can. Dan, you go over an' stand by the window. I want you to keep at least ten paces apart, an' please don't fire 'til ye get the signal. I'm goin' to give a prize for the simplest weddin' that ever took place in Pointview,' I says. 'It will be five hundred dollars in gold for the bride. Don't miss it.'

"'The marriage will occur at noon,' says Lizzie. 'There'll be nothing but simple morning frocks. The girls can wear calico if they wish. No jewels, no laces, no elaborate breakfast.'

"'An' no presents, but mine, that cost over five dollars each,' I says.

"An' that's the way it was—like old times. No hard work wasted in gettin' ready, no vanity fair, no heart-burnin', no bitter envy, no cussin'

147

about the expense. There was nothing but love an' happiness an' goodwill at that wedding. It was just as God would have a wedding, I fancy, if He were the master o' ceremonies, as He ought to be.

"They are now settled on a thousand acres o' land here in New England. Dan has eight gangs o' human oxen from Italy at work for him getting in his fertilizers. He rides a horse all day an' is as cordy as a Roman gladiator. Do you know what it means? Ten thousand like him are going into the same work, the greed o' the middleman will be checked, an' one o' these days the old earth 'll be lopsided with the fruitfulness of America."

VII

EARLY in June I was invited to
the wedding of Miss Betsey
Smead and the Honorable Socrates
Potter. Miss Betsey had inherited a
large estate, and lived handsomely in
the Smead homestead, built by her
grandfather. She was a woman of
taste and refinement, but, in defer-
ence to Socrates, no doubt, the in-
vitations had been printed in the
office of the local newspaper. There
could have been no better example
of honest simplicity. The good news
sent me in quest of my friend the

lawyer. I found him in Miss Betsey's library. He was in high spirits and surrounded by treasures of art.

"Yes, I'm in luck," he began. "Miss Betsey is a dear soul. We're bound to be happy in spite of all this polished brass an' plate an' mahogany. There's nothin' here that I can put my feet on, except the rugs or the slippery floor or the fender. Everything has the appearance o' bein' more valuable than I am. If it was mine I'd take an axe an' bring things down to my level. I'm kind o' scairt for fear I'll sp'ile suthin' er other. Sometimes I feel as if I'd like to crawl under the grand pyano an' git out o' danger. Now look at old gran'pa Smead in his gold frame on the wall. He's got me buffaloed. Watches every move I make. Betsey laughs an' tells me I can sp'ile any-

thing I want to, but gran'pa is ever
remindin' me o' the ancient law o'
the Smeads an' the Persians."

"Mr. Potter, I owe so much to
you," I said. "I want to make you
a present—something that you and
your wife will value. I've thought
about it for weeks. Can you—"

He interrupted me with a smile and
these gently spoken words:

"Friends who wish to express their
good-will in gifts are requested to
consider the large an' elegant stock
o' goods in the local ninety-nine-cent
store. Everything from socks to sunbursts may be found there. Neck-
laces an' tiaras are not prohibited if
guaranteed to be real ninety-nine-
centers. These days nobody has
cheap things. That makes them rare
an' desirable. All diamonds should
weigh at least half a pound. Smaller

stones are too common. Everybody
has them, you know. Why, the wife
of the butcher's clerk is payin' fifty
cents a week on a solitaire. Gold,
silver, an' automobiles will be politely
but firmly refused—too common, far
too common! Nothin' is desired likely to increase envy or bank loans or
other forms of contemporaneous crime
in Pointview. We would especially
avoid increasin' the risk an' toil of
overworked an' industrious burglars.
They have enough to do as it is—
poor fellows—they hardly get a night's
rest. Miss Betsey's home has already
given 'em a lot o' trouble."

His humor had relieved its press-
ure in the deep, good-natured chuckle
of the Yankee, as he strode up an'
down the floor with both hands in his
trousers pockets.

"Look at that ol' duffer," he went

on, as he pointed at the stern features of grandpa Smead. "Wouldn't ye think he'd smile now an' then. Maybe he'll cheer up after I've lived here awhile."

He moved a couple of chairs to give him more room, an' went on:

"Now, there's Bill Warburton. I supposed he was a friend o' mine, but we had a fight in school, years ago, an' I guess he's never got over it. Anyhow, I caught him tryin' to slip an automobile on me—just caught him in time. There he was tryin' to rob me o' the use o' my legs an' about fifteen hundred a year for expenses an' build me up into a fat man with indigestion an' liver-complaint. I served an injunction on him.

"Another man has tried to make me the lifelong slave of a silver service. He'd gone down to Fifth

Avenue an' ordered it, an' I suppose it would 'a' cost thousands.
Tried to sneak it on me. Can ye
think o' anything meaner? It would
'a' cost me a pretty penny for insur-
ance an' storage the rest o' my life, an'
then think of our—ahem—our poor
children! Why, it would be as bad
as a mortgage debt. Every time I
left home I would have worried about
that silver service; every time the
dog barked at night I would have
trembled in my bed for the safety o'
the silver service; every time we had
company I would have been afraid
that somebody was goin' to scratch
the silver service; an' when I saw a
stranger in town, I would have said
to myself: 'Ah, ha! it may be that
he has heard of our silver service an'
has come to steal it.' I would have
begun to regard my servants an'

many other people with dread an'
suspicion. Why, once I knew a man
who had a silver service, an' they
carried it up three flights to the attic
every night for fifty years. They
figured that they'd walked eleven
hundred miles up an' down stairs
with the silver service in their hands.
The thought that they couldn't take
it with 'em hastened an' embittered
their last days. Then the heirs
learned that it wasn't genuine after
all.

"Of course, I put another injunction upon that man. 'If we've ever
done anything to you, forgive us,' I
said, 'but please do not cripple us
with gold or silver.'"

He stopped and put his hand upon
my shoulder and continued:

"My young friend, if you would
make us a gift, I wish it might be

something that will give us pleasure an' not trouble, something that money cannot buy an' thieves cannot steal— your love an' good wishes to be ours as long as you live an' we live—at least. We shall need no token o' that but your word an' conduct."

I assured him of all he asked for with a full heart.

"Should I come dressed?" was my query.

"Dressed, yes, but not dressed up," he answered. "Neither white neckties nor rubber boots will be required."

"How are Mr. and Mrs. Bill?"

"Happier than ever," said he. "Incidentally they've learned that life isn't all a joke, for one of those little brownies led them to the gate of the great mystery an' they've begun to look through it an' are wiser folks. Two other women are building

orphan lodges on their grounds, an'
there's no tellin' where the good work
will end."

We were interrupted by the en-
trance of Miss Betsey Smead. She
was a comely, bustling, cheerful little
woman of about forty-five, with a
playful spirit like that of Socrates
himself.

"This is my *financée*," said Socrates. "She has waited for me twenty-
five years."

"And he kept me waiting—the
wretch!—just because my grandfather left me his money," said Miss
Betsey.

"I shall never forgive that man,"
said Socrates, as he shook his fist at
the portrait. "An' she was his only
grandchild, too."

"And think how comfortable he
might have been here, and how I've

worried about him." Miss Betsey went on: " Here, Soc., put your feet on this piano seat. Now you look at home."

"When I achieve the reformation of Betsey I shall have a kitchen table to put my feet on!" said Soc., as I left them.

Then I decided that I would send him a kitchen table.

THE END